TALES FROM THE NORTH

Edited By Megan Roberts

First published in Great Britain in 2019 by:

Young Writers
Remus House
Coltsfoot Drive
Peterborough
PE2 9BF
Telephone: 01733 890066
Website: www.youngwriters.co.uk

Book Design by Camilla Davis

SB ISBN 978-1-78988-333-6
Printed and bound in the UK by BookPrintingUK
Website: www.bookprintinguk.com
YB0399C

FOREWORD

Welcome, Reader!

Here at Young Writers our aim is to encourage creativity in children and to inspire a love of the written word. Each competition we create is tailored to the relevant age group, hopefully giving each child the inspiration and incentive to create their own piece of work, whether it's a poem or a short story. We truly believe that seeing their work in print gives pupils a sense of achievement and pride.

For Young Writers' latest nationwide competition, Spooky Sagas, we gave primary school pupils the task of tackling one of the oldest story-telling traditions: the ghost story. However, we added a twist – they had to write it as a mini saga, a story in just 100 words!

These pupils rose to the challenge magnificently and this resulting collection of spooky sagas will certainly give you the creeps! You may meet friendly ghosts or creepy clowns, or be taken on Halloween adventures to haunted mansions and ghostly graveyards!

So if you think you're ready... read on.

CONTENTS

Broadacre Primary School, Hull

Christine Hua Vong (10) 1
Jessica May Rouse (10) 2
Lexy Rebecca Richardson (10) 3
Kieran Miller (10) 4
Lily Mackay (10) 5
Frankie Joy Waller (10) 6
Jasmine Victoria Cook (11) 7
Eboni Grace Skewis (9) 8
Joel Mogg (10) 9
Alice Douglas (10) 10
Jack Nicholas Raymond Waudby (11) 11
Emily Newton (10) 12
Ruby May Palmer (10) 13
Keeley Rogers (10) 14

Hornsea Burton Primary School, Hornsea

Ruby Loveridge (7) 15

James Calvert Spence College, Amble

Rose Henderson (9) 16
Kira Mole (9) 17
Brogan Roebuck (11) 18
Graham Black (11) 19
Grace Marie Elliott (10) 20
Riley Simpson (10) 21
Kenna Cowell (9) 22
Michelle Morrison (9) 23
Myah Goward (10) 24
Riley Moore (9) 25
Lana Ferguson-Wood (11) 26
Myamii Brown (9) 27
Amelia Wilson (10) 28
Harry Dawson (9) 29
Jazmin McNicoll (11) 30
Martha Reynolds (10) 31
Evie Bell (11) 32
Caitlin Davidson (9) 33
William Coleran (10) 34
Jessica Low (9) 35
Rebecca Allan (10) 36
Zoë Ferguson-Wood (11) 37
Jessica Waddell (10) 38
Ella May Keenlyside (9) 39
Joseph Edward McNeill (10) 40
Joshua Yon (9) 41
Grace Holland (10) 42
Aaron Darling (11) 43
Lily-Mae Fraser (10) 44
Harrison Scholes Armstrong (10) 45
Daisy Parker (10) 46
Emma Hobden (9) 47
Scarlet Paterson (9) 48
Evan David McDonough (11) 49
Libby Welsh (10) 50
Alex Georiou (10) 51
Lexie Lowes (9) 52
Jay He (9) 53
Lily May Henderson (10) 54
Katie Dewson (10) 55
Callum Wilson (11) 56
Jack Tait (10) 57
Megan Joyce Bremner (9) 58
Mercedes Thompson (10) 59
Samantha Donnelly (10) 60
Sam Turner-Davison (10) 61

Alexya Jayne Wright (10) 62
Francesca Watkinson (10) 63
Katie Stewart (10) 64
Bethany Wilson (9) 65
Abbie-Jane Wilson (11) 66
Archie Lillie (9) 67
Elise Rodrigues-Morrison (9) 68
Alex Hale (10) 69
Thea Davis (11) 70
Bailey Straker (9) 71
Archie Stefan Henshall (9) 72
Sophie Fogerty (11) 73
Macy Knox (10) 74
Imogen Keenan (10) 75
Caitlyn Mowatt (11) 76
Ava Bremner (9) 77
Isla Lewis (9) 78
Brandon John Ireland (10) 79
Oli Mitchell (10) 80
Jasmin Saunders (11) 81
Brooke Harrison (11) 82
Katie Ferman (9) 83
Evra Nicole Keen (10) 84
Corey Common (10) 85
Oliver Bremner (10) 86
Grace Common (11) 87
Raegan Mckenzie Huntley (10) 88
Ryan Spuhler (10) 89
Sian Coulson (9) 90
Leon Wilson (9) 91
Ayton Baxter (10) 92
Danni Curran (10) 93
Ryan Bunday (10) 94
Olivia Grace McGarvey (9) 95
Jack Thomas Spencer Taylor (11) 96
Jenson Mather (9) 97
Alfie William Stuart Armstrong (9) 98
Jake Morley (10) 99
Jessica Jackson (10) 100
Richard Raine (10) 101
Caitlyn Clough (10) 102
Macey May Henderson (10) 103
Ava Lawson (10) 104
Jessica Lesley Martin (10) 105
Zack Alexander Stott (10) 106
Joshua Harry Pattison (9) 107
Ryan Dewson (9) 108
Marcie Ruth Burge (10) 109
Imogen Ranson (10) 110
Riley Gerrard (9) 111
Jacob Belisle (9) 112
Emily Edwards (10) 113
Felicity Hodgson (10) 114
Ellie Goward (10) 115
Conn Sullivan (10) 116
Emily Martha Clark (11) 117

Luddendenfoot Academy, Luddendenfoot

Marnie Marr (9) 118
Alicia Popps (9) 119
Maisie Hayes (9) 120
Lucas Stringer (10) 121
Lucy Smith (10) 122
Ella Brooks (9) 123

Manston Primary School, Crossgates

Jessica Schofield (10) 124
Lily Swordy (10) 125
Harley James Dews (10) 126
Leah Badcock (11) 127
Lilly Holliday (11) 128
Gracie Leigh Partner (11) 129
Oliver Moran (11) 130
Kasseykylie Kucherera (11) 131
Mia Wood (11) 132
Tyler Emmett (10) 133
Thomas Kilcoyne (10) 134

Parkinson Lane Community Primary School, Halifax

Sameer Ayub (10) 135
Maleeha Naz (10) 136
Haniya Dawood (8) 137
Bisma Moghul (11) 138
Falak Arshid (8) 139
Maryam Bibi (8) 140
Ibrahim Rasul (8) 141
Hudaifa Ali (9) 142
Fizah Junaid (10) 143

Primrose Lane Primary School, Boston Spa

Lucy Harper (10) 144

Pudsey Bolton Royd Primary School, Pudsey

Maryam Yasin (7) 145

Ravensthorpe CE (VC) Junior School, Ravensthorpe

Laibah-Amina Hussain (9) 146
Simran Shakoor (10) 147
Rida Rehman (9) 148

Saltersgate Junior School, Scawsby

Tiffany Robson (10) 149
Olivia Hardy (11) 150
Phoebe Cooper (11) 151

Southroyd Primary School, Pudsey

Scarlett Anne Pattinson (8) 152
Connor Reece Kisby (9) 153
Jamie Lucas O'Brien (8) 154
Jayden Barraclough (8) 155
Evie Mason (9) 156
Rose Janani (8) 157

St Michael's CE Primary School, Dalston

Ebony Dickinson (10) 158
Lucy Olivia Bowie (10) 159
Megan Smith (11) 160

St Patrick's Catholic Primary School, Elland

Ellie Baimbridge (10) 161

St Patrick's CE Primary School, Endmoor

Alfie Hunter (10) 162
Erin Munford (9) 163
Bethany Taylor (11) 164
Oliver Sanday (10) 165
Ethan Kearsley (10) 166
Rhys Newby-Bush (10) 167
Daniel Horrigan (10) 168
Jess Wilson (11) 169
Ben Morris (9) 170
Ella Allan (10) 171
Abby Mason (10) 172
Nathan Barnabas Galbraith (10) 173
Sophie Tubbs (9) 174
William Taylor (9) 175

Three Lane Ends Academy, Castleford

Charlotte Olivia Hawkin (11) 176

West Road Primary School, Moorends

Loretta Knott (9) 177
Milena Bury (9) 178

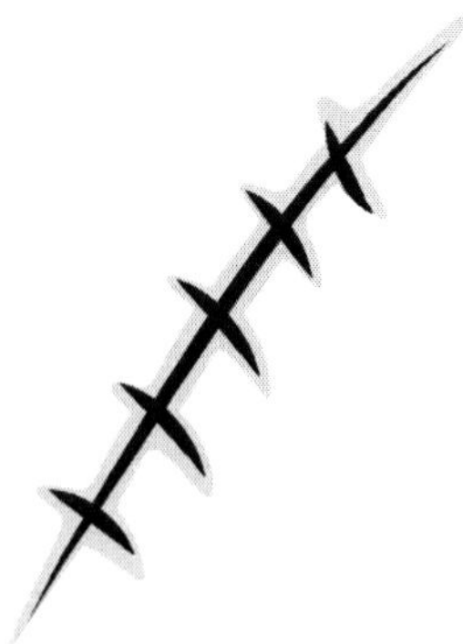

THE SPOOKY SAGAS

MY DREAM HORROR

"Behind you!" the voice sang. "Behind you!"
I sneaked a peek and the face was horrifying.
"Found you!" it screeched.
I screamed. The face had bloody, bedraggled hair with spikes and bloodshot eyes. Suddenly, three slashes appeared on my forearm. Blood, bones... "Help!"
The lights switched off, a blood-red light appeared under her eyes and face. The result was horrifying. Then, I realised that she didn't have eyes, only bloody eye sockets. Her smile was like a psycho smile and absolutely terrifying.
I woke up. "Behind you!"
"Who are you?" I asked. "Hello? Hello? Help me!"
This wasn't a dream...

Christine Hua Vong (10)
Broadacre Primary School, Hull

THE LOST BAT

Once, there lived a bat called Batty. It was Halloween night. "Mama! I'm going around the neighbourhood!" exclaimed Batty.
"Okay, be back at midnight!" replied Mama Bat.
At midnight, Batty said, "I should head home," clearly exhausted. The curious little bat started flying home but got lost.
"Oh no!" shouted Batty, worried. Across the street, a girl called Alina heard the commotion and decided to help.
"There's a big bat over-" started Alina, but she was cut off by Batty.
"Mama!" cried Batty, happy to see his mum again. "Is it okay if I stay with Alina?"

Jessica May Rouse (10)
Broadacre Primary School, Hull

WINTER'S NIGHTMARE

One frosty night, a withered cottage came to view: Lesley's nanna's home. But, today, the door was open with bloodstained hands smeared on it. "Nanna? Are you okay?" Lesley whispered quietly.
As she peered through the door, a dead body lay across the floor. "Nanna!" screamed the girl.
Suddenly, a blood-covered hand reached for her. "Hello Lesley," calmly spoke the strange figure.
It was a doll! As she spoke, she cried, "Your nanna tried to kill me. In return, I will kill you!"
"Argh!" the girl screamed, then it all went silent...

Lexy Rebecca Richardson (10)
Broadacre Primary School, Hull

REAL?

I awoke in the night. I was somewhere new. My body ached all over. I was downright terrified! My mind turned blank, so I did the dumbest thing imaginable: "Hello?" For some reason, I screeched out the 'o' like a ghost. I stepped forwards and heard a click. *Textbook*, I thought. I had gone into a creepy house and was locked in with creaks everywhere! There was a creepy man stood in the corner, whispering mine, Mum's, Dad's and someone else's name. I looked in the mirror...
I was a ghost! I'd died... "Car crash," he whispered in my ear...

Kieran Miller (10)
Broadacre Primary School, Hull

THE GHOST GIRL WHO WANTED A FRIEND

There once was a girl called Gabbi, but she wasn't just an ordinary girl, she was a ghost! One morning, her mum said she could finally go to a ghost school and make some friends. So, that morning, she walked to Ghost School and said to a group of girls, "Do you want to be my friend?"
Unfortunately, they just screamed and ran away. Just as Gabbi walked away, another ghost girl just like her appeared with a smile on her face and whispered, "Hello, I'm Molly."
Gabbi smiled and thought to herself, *finally, a new friend just for me.*

Lily Mackay (10)

Broadacre Primary School, Hull

THE BOY CALLED JOHN!

Tonight is the night that John has been waiting for... Halloween! This year, John was showing his friends that he could go in the haunted house all by himself. All of his friends' big brothers and sisters had gone in and seen a ghost, but he didn't believe them.
Off he went! John stepped inside. Suddenly, a chair in the corner fell. John hesitated. "Just the wind..."
The dusty chandelier swung. John ran, but ghosts jumped out and grabbed him! He wiggled and squirmed. *Crash! Bang!*
John woke up and it was just a dream!

Frankie Joy Waller (10)
Broadacre Primary School, Hull

THE ABANDONED ATTIC

One ordinary day, there was an innocent, young girl. The clock struck 10pm, she heard voices while in bed. She didn't recognise them so she tiptoed into her parents' room; they were asleep.

In the morning, she asked her dad if he could go in her room to check. He agreed and found unusual, mind-muddling discoveries. He discovered a letter which read the date of 1945 and all it said was, 'I miss my brother and wife. Store their ashes in the attic...'

The whispers continued until it got too much and the family moved house.

Jasmine Victoria Cook (11)

Broadacre Primary School, Hull

THE MYSTERY OF THE MISSING GIRL AND HER FRIENDS

Once upon a time, on a moonlit night, a girl went out on a chilling trail with her beloved friends. They wandered the old trails and found their worst nightmare. They wanted to go home.
They came up to some extremely eerie-looking trees and one said, "We're your worst nightmare!"
Another tree kindly greeted them by saying, "Hello children."
Suddenly, a blood-dripping vampire came out of nowhere and said, "Mwahahaha!"
Charlotte ran away and went home to her mum and dad. They all went to bed.

Eboni Grace Skewis (9)
Broadacre Primary School, Hull

MONSTER HOUSE

Once upon a time, there was a terrifyingly spooky house called the Monster House. It was full of lots of horrifying monsters who weren't very friendly at all!
One day, a little boy called Joel was wandering around a dark, spooky forest filled with loud noises and bugs. Suddenly, he spotted the giant house in the distance, so he stopped for a while and then strolled inside.
As Joel wandered inside, a huge army of zombies ran after him. As quick as a flash, Joel hid under the bed, then he ran out the door, never to be seen again.

Joel Mogg (10)
Broadacre Primary School, Hull

LURKING

One dark, Halloween night, a trick-or-treater walked up to a strange house. It was haunted! As he walked up, the door flung open! He stepped inside and the door slammed behind him. He trudged up the stairs where a note was waiting for him. It read, 'He who finds this note must go into the attic and keep the lights off'. He did what the letter told him to do: turn the lights off. He saw a figure getting closer. Something was in its hand. The boy was terrified. The figure stared and slowly said, "I've found you!"

Alice Douglas (10)
Broadacre Primary School, Hull

GHOULY GHOSTS

At midnight, the nightmares come out to play, you can't imagine the horrors that would shock your friends! One boy called Kai walked down the street, scared as he knocked on the door. *Ding! Dong!* It was midnight.
Kai fell in fear as midnight was the ghouly ghost hour. Kai ran home as fast as he could, but it was too late. His legs were aching and his arm was frozen as a dark ghost rose from its grave. Kai saw it coming closer. He started to shake. "You will be with us now," said the ghost angrily, snarling...

Jack Nicholas Raymond Waudby (11)
Broadacre Primary School, Hull

ONCE UPON A TIME!

Once upon a time, there was a family (Lola, Deric, Lily and Edward) but, unfortunately, they were cursed to die whenever they saw someone dance. When Edward was a teenager, Lily died because Lola (her mother) danced! Now, twenty years later, Edward has his second job. Lola died later because Deric, her husband, danced! Edward and his father went on a walk. It was Halloween and they saw the undead! The dead person danced and Deric dropped to the ground, dead. Edward ran to a nearby food place and stabbed himself...

Emily Newton (10)
Broadacre Primary School, Hull

THE MONSTER IN THE FOREST

Once, there was a child who went trick or treating in the forbidden woods. There was a witch's house in there and the witch turned him into a monster. As moonlight struck, the terrifying monster came back and cut down trees. The witch had to leave so the forest was abandoned.

Some trick-or-treaters went in and, as they were about to knock on the house, they started sinking in the mud! The monster was pulling them under! They became his minions until the witch came back and the children were never seen again!

Ruby May Palmer (10)
Broadacre Primary School, Hull

DEAD'S NIGHT DREAM

On the day of the dead in 2017, it began: Halloween! You may think it's not that scary, but think again, for this little girl it is more of a trick than a treat. On this day, she had stepped into the wrong house! No one knew what lay inside this house. There was a mad scientist who wanted to do an experiment with knives on her, which she knew would lead to blood. He did the experiment and she died.
She woke with a start. There he was again with a knife. Nowhere was safe!

Keeley Rogers (10)
Broadacre Primary School, Hull

ZOMBIE AND PUMPKIN

Once upon a spook, there was a zombie. His friend was called Pumpkin. One day, they had a fight about who was the scariest, so the next day, Zombie came with fake blood. "I'm scarier than you now!" said Zombie.
The next day, Pumpkin came in ripped clothes and said, "I bet I'm scarier than you!"
Then, both of them thought the fight was silly. They were sorry, so they went out together to kill humans and animals. They loved to do that, so they all lived happily ever after. Well, not the weird humans and stinking, smelly animals!

Ruby Loveridge (7)
Hornsea Burton Primary School, Hornsea

MOTHER'S SPIRIT

One dark and scary night, something dreadful happened. You're just about to find out what! Clara and her mother (Liz) dashed down the harsh area of empty cobwebs, broken branches where a murderer lived. "Mother!" Clara screamed. "Will we get out of this awful place?"
Clank! Something heavy stepped in front of them. There stood the most dangerous murderer in the forbidden forest. *Bang!* He shot a greasy bullet into the air. *Bang!* again, but this time, it pierced Liz's skin! "Run!" she choked uneasily.
Suddenly, Liz reappeared as a transparent ghost. This surprised Clara. "Mother's spirit," she whispered...

Rose Henderson (9)
James Calvert Spence College, Amble

THE GREEN GLOWING STONE!

Ben and Beany (Ben's teddy) stepped into the house. Beany was popping out of Ben's backpack. The house was full of china dolls that always stared at anyone who walked into the house. Ben saw something moving. It growled quietly, "Come over here!"
It was a dark, terrifying voice. "Who's there?" asked Ben, his voice trembling.
Suddenly, he saw a green, sparkling stone on a string. "Put the necklace on Beany. No talking," commanded the voice.
Ben put the necklace on Beany. There was silence. Then, something fell, then more silence. Something moved. "Thank you, Ben!" Beany suddenly said...

Kira Mole (9)
James Calvert Spence College, Amble

THE STRANGE ENCOUNTER

On a dark day in December, the only light came from a full moon as I hurried past the ancient church attached to a graveyard. Dark shadows swirled around me until a moonlit beam showed the outline of a boy. I called out to him, "Are you okay?"

He slowly turned and said, "I'm fine."

"What's your name?" I asked.

"My name is Thomas Wintersun."

"Are you alone?"

"No, I'm with my family," he sighed. Suddenly, a cloud covered the moon. When the light returned, Thomas was gone. I turned to the gravestone - 'Here likes the Wintersun family'...

Brogan Roebuck (11)

James Calvert Spence College, Amble

THE VAMPIRE'S WORDS

Once upon a time, there was a boy called David. He decided to explore an abandoned castle. He went up to the front door, then he opened the drawbridge. He walked into the kitchen. Then, he heard a noise upstairs, so David went upstairs to investigate. David slowly crept up the stairs. "Hey there David."
"Who said that?" gulped David.
"It's me, the friendly vampire."
"Not you again!" replied David.
"Hee hee hee!"
David ran down the stairs ran out the door, sprinted through the woods. *Boom!* The vampire reached out and grabbed David. "No!"

Graham Black (11)
James Calvert Spence College, Amble

HAUNTED GAME

Cherry and Diamond were playing in the house one day and Cherry found a weird game called Devil Chase. Cherry shouted for Diamond so they could play, but Cherry said it wasn't a good idea. Diamond really wanted to play, so she opened the box and, *bang!* It sounded like someone was downstairs. *Bang!*
Cherry went downstairs and there was blood everywhere. *Bang!* She went upstairs and hid. Diamond screamed, "Argh!"
Bang! Bang! Bang! Someone was coming upstairs. She found Cherry and she was killed as well as Diamond. Their mum came home to find that they were both dead.

Grace Marie Elliott (10)
James Calvert Spence College, Amble

SPIRITUAL KIDNAP

As two boys woke up in the middle of nowhere, they looked at the bottom of the old bed. There it was, a clown and a jester. "Argh!"
They were grabbed and made to be quiet. Their mum called, "Honey! Tea's ready!"
The jester ignored her. The boys said, "Hey! That's our mom!"
"Don't be afraid," said the clown. Then, he said, "You're afraid!"
"Please stop!"
Then, they disappeared into thin air. The boys then ran but one tripped and got pulled to a nearby sewer. "Ron!" said Oliver.
Then, Oliver was kidnapped...

Riley Simpson (10)
James Calvert Spence College, Amble

A SCARY STORY

Alice was in a huge forest. Suddenly, she heard screaming, branches snapping. A man was trying to kill her. She walked into an abandoned mansion and saw a skull in a jar. She knew it was weird. The man was hiding so he could watch her. Her eyes were shut tightly. She knew something wasn't right. There wasn't anyone here. It looked like people were disappearing. She started crying, "Mum, where are you?"
The man said, "Hello little girl. What are you doing here?"
Alice phoned her mum. He grabbed her phone.
"Eek!" she screamed.
"Now I've got you!"

Kenna Cowell (9)
James Calvert Spence College, Amble

RED BALLOON

"You'll float too! You'll float too!" echoed the voice. Lucy stopped dead. Turning around, she found a horrifying doll. "Come play with Anabell!"

Lucy darted across the hall, panting for breath. Once at the door, Lucy locked it, then sprinted across to the main door. "Come on!" yelled Lucy.

In desperation, she tried ramming herself into the door. She knocked herself out. When she woke up, Lucy noticed blood, guts and other revolting things. Then, screams filled the orphanage and... *Bang!* Suddenly, she saw a red balloon and she was never seen again...

Michelle Morrison (9)
James Calvert Spence College, Amble

LOOK BEHIND YOU!

As me and Stewart walked through the abandoned graveyard, I noticed something was written on the church window. I just couldn't quite work out what it said. Suddenly, Stewart stopped dead. Out of the blue, he screamed, "Run!"
I ran for my life. I heard a blood-curdling scream. "Argh!"
Terrified to look back, I sprinted. Finally, I reached the wrecked church. Over and over again, I heard the scream. I was shivering and had tears dripping down my face. I wondered what it could have said on the window. It'd said 'Look behind you' painted in bright red blood...

Myah Goward (10)
James Calvert Spence College, Amble

REAGON AND ASHTON DIE, SO DOES LEE

Reagon and Ashton were playing a dare game. Ashton dared Reagon to touch Lee's grave.
"Okay," said Reagon.
Reagon suddenly felt the ground shake, the pebbles on the path shot up like rockets. Then, a hand appeared from the ground. As it came out, its bottom came off. "Argh! Zombie, run!" screamed Ashton and Reagon, running as fast as their little legs could carry them.
They ran into a hospital. A tiny voice said, "You'll float too!"
It was a clown and... *Bang!* Reagon and Ashton were never to be seen again. Even Lee's zombie was killed!

Riley Moore (9)
James Calvert Spence College, Amble

GOODNIGHT

She didn't believe the rumours, the house's reputation. She'd been warned about the stories: how each inhabitant had supposedly died on night seven, 11pm, in the deepest, darkest corner of the basement. Every night, she'd creep down to the spine-chilling room and mutter, "Goodnight," under her breath. Silence. On night seven, at 11pm, she sneaked down the spiral staircase again and said goodnight. She waited patiently for a few seconds before making her way back upstairs. Only one thing could be heard as she exited the basement: a soft, ghostly, "Goodnight..."

Lana Ferguson-Wood (11)
James Calvert Spence College, Amble

Nobody Knows It Was An Abandoned Circus

One dark, misty night, the twins discovered a circus. It was like the circus was expecting them. They loved clown houses.
As they entered, there were creepy clown statues, but the twins loved the circus. They heard something and they shouted, "Popcorn!" It disappeared before their eyes. "Ohh..."
They suddenly screamed. Myamii awoke, she knew where the twins had gone, so she ran to the clown house. The clown was attacking the twins. Myamii kicked the door down and defeated the evil clown. Myamii got the twins and they never went back there again. Myamii was a hero!

Myamii Brown (9)
James Calvert Spence College, Amble

FRANKENSTEIN

As midnight fell, Frankenstein walked through the dark, gloomy forest. Nearby, in the abandoned churchyard, lay all the predators waiting to catch their prey. As Frankenstein reached the church gate, he gently pushed it open. Stumbling along the path, Frankenstein walked up towards the door. He pushed the door and tripped inside the door and the door closed behind him.
As he walked through the corridor, every door he passed looked mysterious. When he got to the next room, he opened it. It was like an escape room or a puzzle room. Frankenstein was trapped forever and couldn't escape...

Amelia Wilson (10)
James Calvert Spence College, Amble

THE DECISION

Two men called Jeff and Josh were in their car, driving. They were minding their own business when they drove past a house with a broken door and holes in the roof and walls. "I wonder what that could be?" said Josh.

"I can't see, it's the middle of the night and it's foggy," replied Jeff.

"I want to go see what it is," said Josh.

"No, you don't need to see what it is, you're a grown man," replied Jeff. Josh had a frown on his face. "Okay, let's go and see what it is," said Jeff.

"Yay!"

Harry Dawson (9)

James Calvert Spence College, Amble

THE DREADED FOREST OF HORROR!

The slimy, green, neon ghost dripped bright neon goop all around the forest. The forest lake wasn't crystal clear, it was blood red. The vampire's food was ready at the bloody lake. The wolves howled with hunger, the green, slimy ghost sprinkled 'scarecrow horror' on the scarecrows. The scarecrows woke up and got ready to keep their land safe. The slimy, green, neon ghost had teeth like knives. The brutal ghost chuckled with victory. The witches chuckled with the ghost because they'd saved the land. The ghost flew away to the party land to celebrate his only victory.

Jazmin McNicoll (11)
James Calvert Spence College, Amble

BLIND TAG

It was Ella's birthday; Ella was dead. Jemma and Ella were sisters and they loved to play, but not Blind Tag. Ella hated it; Jemma loved it. Jemma, feeling lonely, turned her sister into an imaginary friend. "Maybe just one game of Blind Tag. Ella won't mind, she's an imaginary friend."

She closed her eyes and said, "You can't catch me!"

But, as she was playing in the darkness, she felt a cold hand on her back and Ella's voice say, "Tag."

It really was Blind Tag. She opened her eyes but still couldn't see a thing...

Martha Reynolds (10)

James Calvert Spence College, Amble

THE WORST ADVENTURE EVER

A wolf called Thor was exploring an abandoned house that was rugged and twisted in lots of places. He heard a huge, closed door creak open. Thor stepped in and the door closed. Thor was a fearless wolf who wasn't afraid of anything. His face was all cracked and smashed because he'd been in lots of fights and wars. He kept on hearing really spooky things... *Whoo! Shh! Mmm! Argh!* It got quieter and quieter until it was silent. The house was quiet until... *Bang! Kaboom!* Thor let out a blood-curdling scream. "Argh!"
He ran away very quickly.

Evie Bell (11)
James Calvert Spence College, Amble

MUM? DAD?

On a dark, wintery night, I had just gotten home from a party. "Mum? Dad...? Mum? Dad?"
They were gone. Tears rolled down my cheek, I didn't know what to do. After a while, I decided to go and find them. I called my friends (Holly and Felicity) to see if they would help. They eventually came over to help.
We entered the dark, gloomy woods. It was silent. We heard a horrifying scream. "What was that?" whispered Felicity.
The scream was my parents getting killed! My heart was pounding, my friends were so shocked. What would happen to me...?

Caitlin Davidson (9)
James Calvert Spence College, Amble

THE DOLL'S FAVOURITE OWNER

Bang! The lights started to flicker. The patient in the spooky hospital was quivering and biting her curly fingernails under the bed covers. The patient poked her head out when, finally, she saw the doll on the other side of the window in a red dress. The patient quickly realised it was no ordinary doll, it was her favourite doll as a kid. It was Anais!
She blinked once and *bam*, the doll was right in front of her. "Argh!"
She pushed the doll away and sprinted for her life. The patient looked behind her, Anais was there... "Argh!"

William Coleran (10)
James Calvert Spence College, Amble

THE HAUNTED CASTLE

As Charlie was walking through the dark, spooky woods, he could see a creature with dark, beady eyes. At first, he didn't know where his sister (Ellie) was, but then he realised that Ellie was behind him. Then, Charlie asked, "Ellie? What should we do?"
"I don't know," said Ellie, so off they went, hugging each other all the way through the forest. They came across a haunted castle. They decided to walk into the haunted castle, but they heard somebody screaming from the inside of the haunted castle. Then, they saw a dead zombie in the castle...

Jessica Low (9)
James Calvert Spence College, Amble

THE EVIL BLOB, UP A NOSE

There was a little blob who lived up a little girl's nose. She wasn't the luckiest because Blob wasn't the nicest blob. One day, he got sick of doing all the boring tricks, so he did three evil ones. His first trick was to give her a nosebleed with his sharp teeth. *Cut!* "Ow!" she screamed. His second trick was to stamp on her nose with his robot-like feet. For his final trick, he was going to cut off her nose with his nails! *Chop!* "Argh!" she cried. "My nose is gone!"
Plop! Then, she suddenly died!

Rebecca Allan (10)
James Calvert Spence College, Amble

THE MIRROR

She woke with a start, eyes wide, sweat dripping down her head. It was deathly silent in her dark, cold house. The little girl glanced out the window to see pure darkness. Her eyes were fixed to an ancient, golden mirror. She sank into her bed with fear as the thud of a heartbeat moved the mirror's dirty glass.
She eventually, cautiously tapped the mirror. The glass instantly shattered; two ghostly arms seized the girl and a blood-curdling scream echoed round her room. An eerie figure stepped out the mirror and onto Earth with beady, menacing eyes filled with evil.

Zoë Ferguson-Wood (11)
James Calvert Spence College, Amble

A SPOOKY SHOCK!

The day Jerry and his father visited his grannie at the graveyard, they were never to be seen again. It all started when Jerry and his dad went to the graveyard to put some flowers on the grave. As they went to place the flowers down, a strange hole appeared in the ground. The hole sucked them both in, they didn't know what was happening.
"Help!" Jerry screamed as his father was getting sucked into a different world. Then, Jerry came flying through. They both woke up in Jerry's grannie's old, forgotten house. They still lie there to this day...

Jessica Waddell (10)
James Calvert Spence College, Amble

DARK NIGHT

It was November, Friday 13th, 2019. I was in a dark tree house in my garden for the night, nothing to do. It was dark. My friend went to get something out of the house. I felt something grab me. I got scared, so I looked behind me. There was a tall man, no face, long arms and legs. I shouted.

My dog came running outside. The man ran into the forest. My friend ran out the house, saying, "Ella! Come here!"

"What?"

"I heard you shouting!"

"There was a man. I see him, he's right there! Help me now, please!"

Ella May Keenlyside (9)

James Calvert Spence College, Amble

MURDER MAYHEM

Bang! A colossal flash of lightning hit the top of an abandoned, smashed up castle while my brother vanished into thin air. I roamed around until a blood-curdling scream came from the south side of the forest. I dashed into a gloomy castle to stay safe.
When I realised there were puddles of blood everywhere, I was speechless. I couldn't call the police unless I found a socket to charge my phone. I realised it was Warkworth Castle, the scariest castle ever. The dry blood on the wall said, 'His skeleton will lie in the chambers forever'...

Joseph Edward McNeill (10)
James Calvert Spence College, Amble

THE DOLL

Once upon a time, there was a middle school called James Calvert. *Bang!* "Argh!" screamed the students and, at that moment, we heard an announcement on the speakers.
We heard the teacher say there was a lockdown but, at that very moment, we heard the door open. "Here's Lucky!" said a voice. "Oh, are we playing hide-and-seek...? Found you!"
The doll found Aiden and killed him. We tried to sneak out, but it caught us. We made a run for it. I went with Jacob and Harry. We ran into each other and fell. It saw us...

Joshua Yon (9)
James Calvert Spence College, Amble

THE CURSE OF THE FOREST

A dark, spooky forest was surrounded by myths and legends about those who dared to enter, never to return. As I walked into the deserted forest, something felt eerie. Then, a creepy ritual song was sung by forgotten, missing children with unsolved cases. "Hello? Who's there?" I whispered.

Suddenly, I felt a rock on my back. It was a warning. I ran as fast as I could have ever dreamed, but to only have my eyes locked shut. The next morning I woke up, but my surroundings weren't the same as I was turned into a photo for centuries!

Grace Holland (10)

James Calvert Spence College, Amble

THE HAUNTED CASTLE

On one cold, dull Halloween night, a young boy called Callum lived in a castle. Callum was dressed in a green ghoul costume. All of a sudden, the doorbell rang. Callum went to answer it. It was 6pm.

Callum got to the door. There was nobody there, but there was a note from Callum's favourite pantomime: 'He's behind you'. Callum turned and faced the horrible, green-faced ghoul standing in front of him. He fell back and closed his eyes tightly like his life depended on it.

Callum opened his eyes. It was all a dream! It was all over.

Aaron Darling (11)

James Calvert Spence College, Amble

I'M COMING TO GET YOU!

Bang! I sprinted up to the door of the house. I could hear blood-curdling screams the second I walked in. I looked at the bed and there was a woman in a lace ballgown, crying. "Are you alright, Alice?" I questioned.
I got no reply. Nervously, I looked behind me. She wasn't there. I looked at the dusty mirror and it had the words 'Look behind you!' in what looked like blood.
As I turned around, a hand grabbed me and pulled me to the ground. Something or someone didn't want me here. It wanted me out for good...

Lily-Mae Fraser (10)
James Calvert Spence College, Amble

SILENT MURDER

On a dark, gloomy, stormy day, two boys were exploring the woods. Then, a storm started tearing down trees. They saw a house in the distance that was abandoned. It was spooky inside the house. They started hearing ghosts and zombie sounds. Suddenly, Haunter flew inside Bill and murdered him quickly. Tyler ran for it. He was lost in the mansion and got chased onto the roof! Tyler had one option: jump! So he did.

One year later, his body was found at the house. Bill's body was buried at the house. Tyler's body vanished the day of the funeral!

Harrison Scholes Armstrong (10)
James Calvert Spence College, Amble

WE'RE BACK

Something sinister was going to happen at midnight. I woke up to dead animals each morning; who was doing this?
Last night was strange, I was lying in bed, quaking with fear. Suddenly, I heard a blood-curdling scream coming from the farmhouse. Running, my legs shaking, I saw a cow lying lifeless with fresh blood oozing from its heart. I gasped in horror.
All of a sudden, there was the body of the dead cow looming towards me, its blank eyes staring at me. Then, more dead animals softly drifted towards me. I screamed as I took my last breath...

Daisy Parker (10)
James Calvert Spence College, Amble

THE GRAVEYARD

My eyes were dreamy and I was falling asleep. A hole appeared in my bed, so I fell right through it. *Bump!* I landed in a graveyard surrounded by a dark, dense forest. Suddenly, black outlines ran behind the nearest trees. The figures with high, red collars emerged out of the trees, singing a death song.
As the monster-vampires came closer, I tried to scream, but no sound came out. I closed my eyes, waiting for my death, waiting for those horrid teeth, but nothing happened. I was super scared. I felt their teeth scrape me then, I woke up!

Emma Hobden (9)
James Calvert Spence College, Amble

BROTHER'S MISSING

A few days ago, my brother went missing. It was a strange mystery. The last time I saw him was deep in the gloomy forest he just vanished. I decided to look for my little brother. My heart was pounding like crazy. As I wandered out into the misty forest, I shouted, "Dan! Dan!" There was no reply. As I crept more into the forest, I spotted a spooky-looking cemetery. *Could he be in there?* I thought. When I went in, the ground started to shake and something came out. "Argh!" I screamed.
He was never seen again...

Scarlet Paterson (9)
James Calvert Spence College, Amble

THE ABANDONED HOUSE

One dark night, four little children went out trick or treating. They knocked on a few houses before they came to this one house; on the gate it said, 'Enter at your own risk!' One of the children said, "I don't think we should go in here. We've already got loads of sweets." Another one said, "Stop being a wimp!"

So they went in and, when the door opened, there was no one there. They went in. The door closed behind them. They looked right, then left, they saw nothing. They were never seen ever again...

Evan David McDonough (11)
James Calvert Spence College, Amble

HAUNTED ADAMS

The Adams just moved into Hill House. People said it was haunted, it was! The Adams' parents, Chris and Jill, had three children: Anthony (the oldest), Hedi (the middle) and Jack (the youngest). Jack was playing in his room when the closet door opened. Hedi was passing, so he called her in and she went into the closet. It shut when she went in and it locked. He called, "Mum! Dad! Anthony!" They all came in and, suddenly, the door opened. Hedi was on the floor. She grunted. Hedi had turned red and black... a demon! They screamed.

Libby Welsh (10)
James Calvert Spence College, Amble

PUMPKINHEAD

One spooky night, a man called Max went to the abandoned, haunted castle. The moon was full and it was a bloody red. Suddenly, Max got his head shot off by a psycho killer and the killer replaced his head with a pumpkin.
Another person ran into the castle and he didn't know he was a victim.
Pumpkinhead was waiting in the corner for his prey. He was watching, waiting and listening. He grabbed the victim and stabbed him. He was bleeding and he ran. Pumpkinhead chased him out of the castle, out of the woods and Pumpkinhead walked away...

Alex Georiou (10)
James Calvert Spence College, Amble

A SLEEPOVER

I was having a sleepover with my bestie, Ava. We had a pizza while watching a movie. We told a story and then, strange things happened. The windows slammed shut and the door creaked open and we hid under the bed. We heard footsteps creeping around the room. The person started knocking stuff off the tables and shelves. Then, the person climbed out of the bedroom window and hopped over the gate.
Me and Ava got out from under the bed. There was smashed glass everywhere. We started cleaning up and then went to bed after locking the windows...

Lexie Lowes (9)
James Calvert Spence College, Amble

THE BREAKDOWN

On a dark, haunted night, the dead awoke. We ran for our lives, away from the zombies. We ran into a dusty, creepy cottage. The pack of us went inside, seeing something we'd never seen before: a cauldron with a bubbly, hot acid inside. I heard knocking on the cottage door, the undead were coming. We panicked, trying to find a magical exit.

Soon, we voted to build wooden barriers which would keep us alive for a few days. The days passed. What could we do? We'd run out of everything. We were doomed. The undead broke down the door...

Jay He (9)

James Calvert Spence College, Amble

AND THEN THERE WAS ONE

While looking for Alfie, I came across an abandoned mansion. It was dirty and the door slightly open. As I pushed the door, it creaked loudly, startling me. I took a deep breath and continued inside. It was dark, dusty and covered in cobwebs. Beams of light shone through cracked windows. I entered what seemed to be a kitchen, it was chillingly cold. I looked up and froze with fear: Alfie was hanging from the ceiling. As he started to swing from side to side, I turned and ran, heading for the outside when, suddenly, I was grabbed from behind...

Lily May Henderson (10)
James Calvert Spence College, Amble

THE SWITCH GHOST

They stopped outside the haunted house, not wanting to go inside. The door creaked slowly as they opened it, dark shadows filling the cold air. They went inside the freaky house, there were bugs everywhere! They found a cold, rusty bed and had a rest before looking for something scary to do.

Then, the lights started going on and off and all they could see was a white thing coming closer and closer towards them. They tried to switch the lights off, but it didn't work. They all got taken away somewhere, but no one knew where they were!

Katie Dewson (10)
James Calvert Spence College, Amble

THE CLOWN

A group of teens were walking in the spooky forest at midnight. They came across a sign saying, 'Clown above this point'. They went in because they didn't believe there was one but, when they went inside, they heard a creepy voice echoing through the forest. Then, they heard a scream, so they looked at each other. Someone was gone! There was another scream. They ran quickly and found their dead friend. Then, they were gone. Behind them was the spooky clown. They were never seen again. After that day, no one went into the forest...

Callum Wilson (11)
James Calvert Spence College, Amble

THE KILLER

As Jake the eleven-year-old was running away from his friends, he was charging towards the Ice Scream woods where whoever entered would never leave. Then, suddenly, Jake saw a speeding shadow moving at the speed of light. He just knew that he was seeing things, but he kept on seeing it many times. He knew it was after him, so he started running from the speedy figure.

It was getting so weird, the trees were moving away from him as he ran. Then, Jake woke up in a creepy position and looked out the window... There was the creepy figure...

Jack Tait (10)

James Calvert Spence College, Amble

BACKED IN THE CORNER!

I woke up from a nightmare and realised it was Halloween. I got changed and went trick or treating. I slowly walked down the colossal, steep hill and found a house. It looked abandoned, but maybe it was just in bad condition. Suddenly, I heard a howl. I decided to run into the run-down place and... I was locked in! I crept further in... What was going to happen to me? "Help!"
Had anyone heard me? I thought somebody heard me. I started to bang on the door. Something started to back me into a corner. "Help me! Please!"

Megan Joyce Bremner (9)
James Calvert Spence College, Amble

GEORGE IN THE FOREST

As George walked into the dark forest, the trees had gnarled branches. Tree stumps tripped him up. His legs trembled as he heard a scream. George knew it wasn't him screaming because he wasn't screaming. Crows screeched, wolves howled. George could hear rustling in the bushes. He was so scared, really scared. He wanted to go home immediately. He was terrified and needed to go home that second.

He came to a big house. It was huge! He hated it there, he wished that he had never gone there because he heard some terrifying screams!

Mercedes Thompson (10)
James Calvert Spence College, Amble

BRIGHTVILLE HOSPITAL

It was a cold night. Mr Mushroom went for some surgery at Brightville Hospital. The next day, everyone was found dead at Brightville Hospital. Mr Mushroom's children went to go and investigate. When they got there, the big window was smashed and the zombies were inside. They got past the zombie that was coming after them, but they were on the roof. They saw their dad, but he had a giant hand. Amelia went to hug him, but then the zombies jumped and the roof fell. All of them were zombies now and, after two years, everyone was a zombie...

Samantha Donnelly (10)
James Calvert Spence College, Amble

THE MUTANT APOCALYPSE

Suddenly, three people walked to an abandoned laboratory and Joe said to Sam, "I dare you to go in there."
Sam said, "Okay."
"Also," Harry said, "I will be right behind you with my wand to protect us in case of any danger."
They went in and they found a bottle with a label on: 'Mutant'. Harry felt slobber fall on him and he turned around. There was a mutant dog and he paralysed it for a second. Then, it chased them and Harry killed it with a spell. But, there was another one...

Sam Turner-Davison (10)
James Calvert Spence College, Amble

THE HAUNTED SCHOOL

It was Halloween night, the clouds were grey, the sky was gloomy. Grace was heading out in a scary devil costume. When she came across a boarded-up school, out of the corner of her eye she saw an old gravestone. The darkness enticed her to go inside...
She crept into the wreck. Grace went into a dusty classroom where there were bones and she heard a noise. She stepped into the back cupboard. The door slammed behind her. Her teeth were chattering and she was shaking like a leaf. She turned on her torch and there was a hideous zombie...

Alexya Jayne Wright (10)
James Calvert Spence College, Amble

IN THE WOODS

One dark and windy night, some kids were staying in the dark, gloomy woods for two nights. Later that night, they found a house far in the woods. They didn't think anyone lived there because the house was all tattered with cracks in the window and tiny holes in the door. They opened the creaky door very slowly and stepped inside. It was dark and it smelled like someone had died. Then, they looked in the hallway and some man was standing there with a knife. He walked towards them, so they ran away. They heard him scream very loudly...

Francesca Watkinson (10)
James Calvert Spence College, Amble

Zomontious

He's a spooky, scary, awful zombie. He lives in a haunted house and hunts brains with his computer brain. One day, he monitors a delicious human, suddenly zapping them with his laser fingers and dragging them into his house of horrors. But, when the zombie eats their brains, they turn into a zombie. He creates a tribe of zombies and is planning to take over the world.
As that zombie is hunting down more innocent humans, they slowly conquer the world. They have 2,808,010 more people to go. We're doomed! Hide under your beds, now!

Katie Stewart (10)
James Calvert Spence College, Amble

THE MAN WHO MURDERS

Mia was on her way to her friend's new house. It was starting to get cold and dark, so she decided to take a shortcut through the dark, damp forest. She was lost and stuck in the middle of nowhere. Out of the shadows came a man and, without saying anything, he escorted her to an old, dark house. On the pavement read 'look behind you'. She was terrified.
She scurried inside and, to her terror, she saw a mason jar with a skull instead of food inside it. Just to be sure, she asked, "What is that thing...?"

Bethany Wilson (9)
James Calvert Spence College, Amble

CREEPY DOLLS

There is this creepy doll called Abbie. She loves to play. When you sleep, she sneaks out the house and stabs people in their legs with her sharp knife. She's very cute when it's light or the morning. In the dark and damp, she's evil. Abbie is a green wolf alpha demon with green ears and tail. Abbie goes out and sucks blood.
"Ah! Blood, the thing I need!"
Then, she goes back home and eats and drinks a bottle of blood, doll body parts and loads of dark dust and wet, sticky skin. She then goes to sleep.

Abbie-Jane Wilson (11)
James Calvert Spence College, Amble

HAUNTED HOUSE IN THE CITY

One fine day, Jasah was parking his car, eating his KFC, when he spotted a haunted house in the dark woods. He finished off his chicken and he went to explore the haunted woods. He saw a dark figure. He walked closer and closer until the dark figure spoke. He said, "Follow me." So, Jasah followed the figure to an underground bunker next to the haunted house. The figure opened the door and threw Jasah inside the bunker. It picked up a bottle saying 'Devil Potion' and it smashed into the bunker. Jasah died.

Archie Lillie (9)
James Calvert Spence College, Amble

CHASED BY CHUBY

In the dead of night, Ellie could see a jet-black, broken mansion. In the dark of the night, Ellie walked towards the broken mansion, through the woods. She couldn't see anything except for her shadow on the muddy ground. As Ellie looked up at the house, she became more scared. She felt a shiver up her spine as she entered the house. She could see a chubby doll with a knife. It wasn't fake. It came running after her. She couldn't believe what she was seeing with her own eyes. She screamed for help, "Argh!"

Elise Rodrigues-Morrison (9)
James Calvert Spence College, Amble

KARL AND THE INFECTED SCORPIONS

It was a dark, starry night. A boy called Karl was walking on a misty street when a light switched on in the abandoned hospital. Karl went up to the hospital and opened the door cautiously. It squeaked. He stepped inside. He went up some steps and heard some zaps from the surgery room. Karl walked in and, to his surprise, he saw a giant, infected scorpion. The scorpion looked at Karl with all of his four, beady eyes. The chase was on.
Karl turned and ran. From nowhere, another scorpion pinned him down. It was all over...

Alex Hale (10)
James Calvert Spence College, Amble

WHITE-EYES

Have you ever met someone who can roll their eyes into the back of their head? Ethan could; his sister hated it! All it took was one push over the edge and he was gone. He was dead but came back. He climbed up the cliff, his eyes pure white. He got to the top and started singing, "My name is White-Eyes, do you want to play?"
Then, one more push and his sister was gone too! Now they roam together, searching for their next victim, all the while singing, "Our names are White-Eyes, do you want to play?"

Thea Davis (11)
James Calvert Spence College, Amble

THE HALLOWEEN HEIST

I was out trick or treating near my friend's estate in Las Vegas. I saw five people dressed in dark clothing with masks on. At first, I thought they were trick-or-treaters, but no, they were heading straight for the bank of Las Vegas. I could hear gunshots and people dropping to the floor, so I called the police. They said they'd be there in ten minutes. When they arrived, the robbers had $10,000,000 in their pockets. The police arrived and saved us all. They were arrested and put in jail for a long, long time.

Bailey Straker (9)
James Calvert Spence College, Amble

DEVIL FRIEND

I went to a shady park with a broken scooter and swings that were squeaky. A werewolf with red eyes popped out from behind a tree. A devil appeared from the shadows. The werewolf belonged to the devil, he was his pet. The devil said, "Do you want to be my friend?"
"Yes," I replied and off we went to his house. We had to go in the back door because he said, "If my parents see you, they'll eat you!"
I didn't listen. I walked straight into the sitting room and his dad saw me...

Archie Stefan Henshall (9)
James Calvert Spence College, Amble

THE FOREST

You and your sister decide to go to the haunted forest down the road. You get in the car and start heading to the forest. You think this is a bad idea, your sister thinks otherwise. The car starts to run out of gas. It's midnight, you're scared, terrified, so your sister goes to get the gas instead.
A few minutes pass and you start to hear tapping. *Tap! Tap! Tap!* A policeman comes to the car and takes you. You look back, your sister hangs from a branch, blood dripping. She's dead, gone forever...

Sophie Fogerty (11)
James Calvert Spence College, Amble

SLENDERMAN AND THE FOREST!

One day, Frankie trudged through an abandoned forest and, all of a sudden, it turned pitch-black. He stepped back and tumbled down a steep hill covered with slippery, crunchy leaves. *Crack!* Frankie shivered. He wondered where he was.

As he stood up, he heard a whisper, "Stay. I won't hurt you."

As the dark figure approached him and stretched its long, wiggly arms, Frankie took a step back again and disappeared into infinity. The long-armed shadow did too. Would this be the end of Frankie?

Macy Knox (10)
James Calvert Spence College, Amble

THE FORBIDDEN FOREST

As she started to dash about the moonlit, creepy forest, she started to hear creepy noises. She was wondering where she could go to get some sort of safety. The scared, lost little girl felt a weird, chilling sensation down her back. She realised seconds later that she had giant scratches up and down her back, hands, arms and legs.

She was scared for her life, so she started to run and, as soon as she did so, she woke up in her home. She had giant, red scratches all over her body! At that moment she was terrified!

Imogen Keenan (10)

James Calvert Spence College, Amble

SPOOKY HOUSE

As me and my scared friends walked up to the haunted, creepy, old, deserted house, I stood there in fear. She opened the creaky door. It was a lady Frankenstein! We screamed so loud, it woke up the neighbourhood. I ran in pure fear. She got my friends.
I ran to another street, it was abandoned. I turned the corner; she was right in front of me with blood running down her face. She grabbed me, pulling me into her damp, dark, haunted house.
I woke up in shock. It was a nightmare. I never dreamed of it again...

Caitlyn Mowatt (11)
James Calvert Spence College, Amble

SLENDERMAN

We entered the dark, gloomy forest. My heart pounded and knees trembled. One friend took the lead and the other was beside me. I was scared. We then heard howls, it was getting dark. We set up camp then went exploring.
As we got deeper into the forest, we saw a small cottage. The door was open, so we crept inside. Now I was really scared because there was blood on the floor and walls. I was sobbing.
We entered one of the rooms and there was the most horrible thing ever. It had no face, tentacles and a body!

Ava Bremner (9)
James Calvert Spence College, Amble

THE VAMPIRE STRIKES

As Elena's friend went home, Elena headed up on the black stage to practise her dancing. She did a bit of the Nutcracker when, suddenly, she heard a noise. She turned around to see nothing but a jet-black bat. She chose to ignore it when, suddenly, there was a movement of dark red curtains. She started to get a bit scared. Then, there was a noise, a bit like footsteps coming towards her. She was now shivering like a leaf. She felt like the music was getting louder. A vampire then bit her right on her warm neck...

Isla Lewis (9)
James Calvert Spence College, Amble

IT

Once upon a time lived a farmer called Bob. Bob was admiring his fields when he heard a bang behind him. But, when Bob looked behind him, there was a scarecrow lying there, face first on the cold, wet floor. When he looked back at his fields, the scarecrow jumped up on him and chased him into an old church. As soon as Bob went into the church, he noticed a light with a loose chain. The scarecrow entered the church soon after and ran towards Bob. Without thinking, Bob shot the scarecrow and chased it. *Splat!*

Brandon John Ireland (10)
James Calvert Spence College, Amble

BEND TILL YOU BREAK

Crash! As Harry hit branches in the dark woods, his heart was racing. Luckily, there was a hospital there to help or he'd be dead. The bad thing was that no one was there except Harry's friend, Milly. He asked her what on earth she was doing there. She said she was chased by a tall man with no face. Harry said he couldn't be far, he'd just been chased by him! Then, there was a strange noise down the hallway. It was too dark to see. Suddenly, the lights went out and there was only a scream...

Oli Mitchell (10)
James Calvert Spence College, Amble

LOVE AT FIRST BITE

The powerful ten-foot giant had a rock body and a red, spiky shell. He had two tongues and was usually found in the dark, abandoned church in the middle of a horrifying, gloomy forest. The monsters were getting ready for a ghoul of a time. Running quickly to the swamp, people ran to survive. The bats screeched and the wolves howled in the light of the moon.
As morning dawned, the monsters finished drinking the fresh blood. They walked away from the swamp, back to their deadly cave to sleep until the next day!

Jasmin Saunders (11)
James Calvert Spence College, Amble

BLOODSUCKING VAMPIRE

It was October 31st, 2018, the night of Halloween, when the first attack happened. I was out with friends going trick or treating when we came to an abandoned, creepy, old house. We knocked on the door and the door opened by itself. Me and my friends went into the abandoned, creepy, old house. Sofia shouted, "Hello? Is anybody in?"
I saw a shadow pass by the creaky, rusted door. I told Sofia, she didn't believe me. I saw it again. It was a witch! We ran upstairs and hid under the bed, waiting...

Brooke Harrison (11)
James Calvert Spence College, Amble

THE ABANDONED CARE HOME

It was Friday the 13th, me and my best friends dared ourselves to have a spooky sleepover in the old, abandoned care home. I know what you're thinking, we're insane! Well, I was the only smart one, so I thought I would bring my German shepherd, Kaiser. He'd help us if someone tried to kidnap us.
We headed into the woods to get to the care home quickly and so no one caught us. We set our sleeping bags up in the care home and decided to tell ghost stories when a loud breathing being was behind us...

Katie Ferman (9)
James Calvert Spence College, Amble

Ghost Girl

It was approximately 9.30pm as Ghost Girl was kidnapping kids. Every time she went into the dark, she glowed. Ghost Girl tried not to wake the three little children, but it was too late. They woke up and heard something. They heard creaking and footsteps and a bang. Their mum and dad heard a scream, so they ran upstairs, but the children were gone! The mum and dad tried to follow Ghost Girl, so Ghost Girl dropped the children. She tried to get them again, but their mum and dad drove away with them quickly!

Evra Nicole Keen (10)
James Calvert Spence College, Amble

THE ABANDONED LAKESIDE

Once there was a boy, he came across an abandoned lakeside. He saw a few torches that had made the trees catch fire. The boy saw some footsteps leading into the lake. He thought someone might be there, watching him. *I'm going to come back tomorrow, it's getting a little creepy...*
The next day, he was going to search properly. He saw the footsteps leading towards the lake. Some went into a bush. He might have to jump into the freezing cold lake to get to the bush to see what was in there...

Corey Common (10)
James Calvert Spence College, Amble

ESCAPE OF THE CENTURY

In a dark forest, there was a giant haunted mansion. In the mansion lived a zombie, a scarecrow and a skeleton. A boy called Jack was walking around in the forest. Then, he walked east and saw the mansion. He opened the door and stepped in. The door creaked and slammed shut behind him. He walked down the hallway. A zombie jumped up behind him, then came the scarecrow and the boy screamed. They took him into a very blurry, dark room and then, they locked the door. After an hour, he escaped and ran back home...

Oliver Bremner (10)
James Calvert Spence College, Amble

THE HAUNTED FOREST

Darkness falls as Alex runs into a spooky, haunted, foggy forest. He stops running in fright. Alex doesn't know where he is. In addition, he carries on walking further until he hears a wolf howling in the distance. Alex is frightened.

Eventually, he can see ahead; he screams and runs as fast as he can. A wolf chases him with excitement. As he's getting chased, he runs into a dead end! What will he do now? Is this the end of Alex?

He wakes up and finds out it was just a nightmare. Or was it?

Grace Common (11)

James Calvert Spence College, Amble

THE LIGHTHOUSE AND THE DOLL!

One summer's day, Ashleigh and her crew were out on a walk. They saw an abandoned house with no lights at all. When they took a step into the garden, they saw a boat and decided they were going to attach it to their Jeep down the road, so they did.
They headed down to the beach with it and saw a tall lighthouse, so they went straight there and, as soon as they got there, an old, creepy doll jumped out. The sky turned back and miserable. From then on, no one went to the lighthouse, it was haunted!

Raegan Mckenzie Huntley (10)
James Calvert Spence College, Amble

THE DISAPPEARING AND REAPPEARING HOUSE

One day, I was going to my house when, suddenly, a house appeared. I thought there wasn't going to be a house. I knocked on the door, but the door was already open. I thought, *someone should've locked it*. I took a little peek in to see if anyone was inside.

When I went in, the door locked me in. I went upstairs to look for a window. I found the window, but it was locked. I looked around the room for the key. I found the key and opened the window, running for my life from the house...

Ryan Spuhler (10)
James Calvert Spence College, Amble

THE VAMPIRE

It was twelve o'clock at night as me and my pet spotted an abandoned graveyard. We opened the gates and entered the cemetery. It was pitch-black, I couldn't see anything at all. I trembled forwards, only to see a swarm of bats fly into my face. Me and Jasper ran away from the bats and saw a bush. Suddenly, there were more. We stood still and, seconds later, a vampire came out of the bush. It headed for us. Jasper and I ran as fast as our legs would carry us. He got closer and closer and closer...

Sian Coulson (9)
James Calvert Spence College, Amble

JAKE'S MYSTERY

As Jake the sixteen-year-old was strolling through a silent forest, he heard a big scream. He darted out the forest, but a haunted house had suddenly appeared in his way in the darkness. Jake darted in but the door slammed shut behind him. Heart pounding, he looked out the window to see what was there... a zombie! He darted upstairs to get away from the zombie, were there more?
He tried to jump in the loft so he didn't get infected by zombies. "I'm going to die," Jake whispered...

Leon Wilson (9)
James Calvert Spence College, Amble

THE ABANDONED HOUSE

As Bob ran through the forest, past the rickety, old, unstable church, past all the trees, bugs, spiders and moths. He ran to the old house on the hill. He ran all the way up the stairs and hid in an old closet filled with fur coats. He then heard a thump as the door slammed. Bob heard footsteps as it came in to get him, but couldn't find him. It was becoming daytime, so the monster vanished into the darkness. Bob then ran back to his home, away from all the beastly, terrible, old, rotten monsters.

Ayton Baxter (10)
James Calvert Spence College, Amble

HALLOWEEN

It was a dark, stormy night on Halloween. I was getting ready for Halloween. I dressed up as a witch. I couldn't wait to get all the delicious candy, so I headed off to get some. But, suddenly, I got lost.
I was in the woods. My heart was pounding, I could hear the leaves rustling, dogs barking. I started to run until there was a house. It was a witch's house. I tried to turn back, but it was too late. They carried me over all the buildings, taking me away...
It was just a dream.

Danni Curran (10)
James Calvert Spence College, Amble

ZOMBIE

One dark night, at 3am, I was praying in an abandoned church. It was nice and peaceful until I heard something. I didn't know what it was so I sprinted away. It heard my footsteps. I went to bed, hoping it was gone.
I went back the next day. I saw a zombie Santa eating Joshua Yon alive. It was very scary. He looked at me. I was really worried, so I ran and hid. He didn't look very nice, just really, really scary. I was there for about half an hour. I was scared. What could I do next?

Ryan Bunday (10)
James Calvert Spence College, Amble

THIS IS HOW I DIED

This is the story of how I died... Every day, I went out on a run past the graveyard, through the street and back. That night, I saw the graveyard as usual and I heard an organ, it was coming from the abandoned house! I walked to leave, but curiosity pulled me towards it.
As I walked towards the door, it slowly creaked open. When I went inside, no one was playing the organ. I walked in further, something grabbed me and pulled me back. It was a zombie! I screamed for help, but no one came...

Olivia Grace McGarvey (9)
James Calvert Spence College, Amble

PALE AS A SHEET

"Where am I?" I asked myself as the lights flickered on and off. I looked down and saw blood dripping from a dead body. I got up but, as I did, something creaked across the floorboards towards me. I picked up a plate and threw it at the beast. It turned out to be a werewolf. I got a silver plate and threw it at the werewolf. The werewolf fell down dead.
I had to get out of this building. By the time I found a window, it was the middle of the night but, outside, there were zombies!

Jack Thomas Spencer Taylor (11)
James Calvert Spence College, Amble

THE AMUSEMENT PARK ORDER

A pizza man got an order at one o'clock, but they were open 24/7, so he went to the address he was given. When he got there, it was an amusement park and he looked everywhere for the person. He heard a loud vibrating sound. He looked behind himself and saw an insane person running at him with a chainsaw. When he saw this, he ran.
He jumped away at the right time and the chainsaw hit the bottom of his shoes. He'd had enough so he ran back and got out of there as quickly as possible!

Jenson Mather (9)
James Calvert Spence College, Amble

MURDER MYSTERY

Once, a little boy called Jim was walking on Halloween. He walked through a dark, dark forest. There were dark trees. In front of the dark, dark trees, there was a dark, dark house, so Jim the trick-or-treater crept into the dark, spooky house. Then, he rang the doorbell. Jim waited and waited and waited until five hours later, a guy came. It was Granny. Granny hit him in the face with a long, thick stick. Would this be the end? This was a nightmare, but unfortunately, Jim died slowly...

Alfie William Stuart Armstrong (9)
James Calvert Spence College, Amble

THE NOT SO FUN SWIM!

One night, two friends went swimming, Molly and Timmy. They went to a lake. The mist cleared, then they saw the lake. They put their towels on a rock nearby and they went in the light blue lake.
Three hours later, they were nearly finished swimming and, at that moment, they saw bubbles from under the lake. They saw a blue light coming up at them. They swam to the shore and then, a blue, fiery man with vines on him appeared and he dragged them under the water. They were never seen again...

Jake Morley (10)
James Calvert Spence College, Amble

THE BAD DREAM

I had just moved into a big house, it was beautiful. It was getting late, so I went to put the TV on and I heard a big bang. It was coming from the loft. I was terrified. There was no one else in the house but me. I went and got the ladders, climbing up to the loft.
It was dark and damp up there. Then, it came from downstairs. I ran to the bathroom, locked myself in, then it was coming upstairs. It came in!
Suddenly, I woke up and there was someone knocking at the front door...

Jessica Jackson (10)
James Calvert Spence College, Amble

THE PUSHER

In the town of Willow Wood, Jack went outside to play. He found the woods in town and went in and, before he knew it, it was dark. He found a hut and heard a cackle. He went inside the hut at his own risk.
Suddenly, a green fog climbed up him. Confused, Jack looked in the dingy mirror. He was a monster! A witch stood at the door and said, "It's nearly midnight. Go to the cliff." When he got there, he pushed her off the cliff. There wasn't a body. Was she dead?

Richard Raine (10)
James Calvert Spence College, Amble

THE HAUNTED HOUSE

In the abandoned village, there was a tall, dark and haunted house with smashed windows. Only brown wood was covering them.
Suddenly, it became midnight and a red light turned on in the creepy house. Out of the blue, there was a scream of a woman!
I ran down the bumpy road, trying not to get run over. The scary, crystal clear ghost was behind me as I looked over my shoulder. I'd never run so fast in my life and I'd never been this scared before! I turned a sharp corner...

Caitlyn Clough (10)
James Calvert Spence College, Amble

THE NEW HOUSE

I slowly crept into my new home, leaving the door open behind me, but not for long... *Bang!* It had shut and I hadn't closed it! I carried on and stumbled to my new room, but there was a doll on my dresser. I got creeped out, so I put it in my mum and dad's bedroom.
Suddenly, in the middle of the night, I heard my door creak open. It was the doll! I screamed, nothing came out because I then realised that another doll was covering my mouth! What a terrible night!

Macey May Henderson (10)
James Calvert Spence College, Amble

HALLOWEEN HORROR

I went out one night on Halloween. There was a full moon too. I went off with my friends to the park in the woods. I went on the swing and I heard something rustling. Then, the swing next to me started to move on its own! Spooky music started playing too. I was so freaked. I told my friends, "Let's go," but they were gone! I started to run, but I heard a deadly scream. There was a girl with a snapped neck and long, black hair. She started chasing me very quickly!

Ava Lawson (10)
James Calvert Spence College, Amble

THE ABANDONED HOTEL

There was a girl called Roxey. Roxey went on a walk and she looked around and she saw a big, angry bull. It had devil horns and red eyes. Roxey found a hotel and ran inside. She found a room and ran inside it. She looked out the window, the bull was there. Roxey hid and she heard banging on the door. Suddenly, the banging stopped. It was silent and peaceful. She left the hotel and ran outside.
Roxey wasn't going out in the forest ever again. Not even going close to one again!

Jessica Lesley Martin (10)
James Calvert Spence College, Amble

THE SHADOW MAN

I crashed my car and all I remembered was someone hitting me on the head. I woke up in a haunted house. I opened the door to a bedroom and noticed another door with a padlock on it. I looked down the corridor and saw a shadow. It looked me in the eye and walked towards me. I ran back in and hid under the bed. It walked in and walked out. I crawled from under the bed and found a padlock key. I opened the door with joy and walked out. The shadow caught up and pulled me back...

Zack Alexander Stott (10)
James Calvert Spence College, Amble

THE UNKNOWN MANSION

One day, a man went to the woods and saw a mansion in the middle. On the top, there were vines. They were so long, you could hardly see the mansion. He walked towards it, there he saw a very scary thing...
On the top of the vines was a vampire! The man screamed and ran for his life, but he couldn't get away. The vampire caught him and took him into the mansion. He was locked in the smallest cupboard. It was very dark. He called out but he was never heard from again...

Joshua Harry Pattison (9)
James Calvert Spence College, Amble

RUN OUTSIDE

In the dead of night, I couldn't get to sleep, so I went to the funhouse. I went all the way to the back. I was glaring at the massive werewolf behind me. I was terrified. I tried to phone my mum, but she didn't pick up the phone. Suddenly, I saw a ghost and a skeleton behind me. They lunged at me, but I managed to outrun the skeleton. I still had the werewolf chasing me. I got stuck at a dead end in the house. The wolf was behind me, so I tried to run outside...

Ryan Dewson (9)
James Calvert Spence College, Amble

FRIDAY THE 13TH

Me and my friends were in the den out in the backyard when we were stopped by my mam, asking if we wanted to sleep out in the dark, gloomy den tonight. Me and my friends thought about it and it was a yes. We told her, "Yes!" for once in our lives.
Hours later, we went to get our things to last the night in the den. It was creepy. We got back, there was someone in the trees with long fingers. We got out a Ouija board but forgot to say goodbye to it...

Marcie Ruth Burge (10)
James Calvert Spence College, Amble

THE HAUNTED HOUSE

Once upon a time, I was in the woods on a dark, windy night. Behind me, I saw a figure in the smashed windows of a haunted house. I got scared and ran inside. Then I heard an old lady banging on the door, screaming. I was very scared. Could she be dead?
Then, something or someone came in so I hid under the bed. All I saw was their feet and then, I saw a knife in its hands. I heard screaming again. Then, the killer kneeled down and got its knife and killed me!

Imogen Ranson (10)
James Calvert Spence College, Amble

FRIDAY 13TH

As I was in the middle of a huge forest, I heard a big, loud noise and I turned around. I saw a big haunted house. A sign said, 'If you come in, you will die!'
After I saw that, I turned around and walked another way. When I went around the corner, a zombie popped up out of nowhere and started chasing me!
As I got away from the zombie that was trying to kill me, I finally got into the house. I was very nervous to see what would happen next...

Riley Gerrard (9)
James Calvert Spence College, Amble

NEVER GO ON THE GHOST DETECTOR APP

I was on the ghost detector app, it was scary. I turned the volume down, it creeped me out and gave me the shivers. I didn't like it, it was scary. I closed my eyes and closed the app. It couldn't be deleted. If you deleted it, a ghost would haunt you.
I was in an abandoned hospital. I heard footsteps on the roof. I had to get out. I wouldn't give up. After ages, I heard voices. They said some scary things. I was scared and I froze forever...

Jacob Belisle (9)
James Calvert Spence College, Amble

IT WAS...

Darkness fell across the school. A muffled scream echoed through the hallway. Red eyes lit up the room. I ran for the door. Suddenly, smoke covered the room and tall, dark figures surrounded me. All I heard was my heartbeat ringing in my ears. The lights turned back on... It was Molly, Daisy, Grace and Misty all laughing, dressed as ghosts, vampires and witches. But, as we were laughing, another scream pierced our ears. This time, it wasn't human...

Emily Edwards (10)
James Calvert Spence College, Amble

HALLOWEEN NIGHT

On Halloween, some people who were scared, fine and excited went into a forest and they were walking for a while. They were tired because it was 11.30 at night. They kept on walking.
They came to a haunted house with wood falling off it, so they went inside and saw lots of dead people on the floor. There were some stairs and, when they went up them, it was squeaky and they saw three people with knives. In two minutes, all the people were dead!

Felicity Hodgson (10)
James Calvert Spence College, Amble

FRIDAY THE 13TH 2004

As I looked out of the window to see a black forest, I was very intrigued. I wanted to play in it, so I grabbed a flashlight and ran into the forest.
It was fun until I got lost and my flashlight died. I tried to walk for a bit, but there was no sign of light or anyone. But, there was someone: a tall man with nothing on his face. He had long tentacles. He grabbed me and flung me into a tree. I could hardly catch my breath and then, he ate me!

Ellie Goward (10)
James Calvert Spence College, Amble

THE OLD CHURCH

Fergus was on his way home. He went past the abandoned church and the glass went *smash!* He turned around and went to investigate. He opened the old door to reveal a cauldron with a potion bubbling. He heard a cackle of laughter and something whizzed past his head. It was a witch on a broom and a ghost priest. He was cornered, the door had gone! The witch hit the boy and the ghost priest jumped on him. He was so terrified, then he woke up!

Conn Sullivan (10)
James Calvert Spence College, Amble

THE CREEPY DEVIL HOUSE!

Once upon a time, there was a man who was a thief. He broke into a massive mansion that a happy couple lived in but, as he was trying to steal something, a box fell on his head and he fell on a spike and it killed him. He turned into a devil because he did something bad.
One night, as the couple came into the house, he scared them and they ran away. To this day, the house is a devil house and nobody went into the house on that street!

Emily Martha Clark (11)
James Calvert Spence College, Amble

THE DOLL IN HER DREAM

I have a sister, she's three and called Maddie. Maddie has this doll that she found in the cellar. I'm concerned about the doll.
It's midnight, I can't sleep. All I can think about is that doll. Then, I hear... "Argh!"
It's coming from my sister's room! I go to see it. The doll has a bat and it wants to kill us. But then, I wake up, it's just a dream! The thing is though, the doll's still there. I wonder, was the dream real or just a dream? I guess I'll have to find out for myself now...

Marnie Marr (9)
Luddendenfoot Academy, Luddendenfoot

THE WORST HALLOWEEN

One day, a teenager called Isla was on her laptop, then there was a sudden knock on the door. Someone had to come to take her to a Halloween party. Then, in the blink of an eye, a witch appeared. She turned boys into gross things and turned girls into witches. Isla was the only person able to save and get rid of the witches.

It got worse because the witch created a dummy that helped the witch turn them into witches or gross things. Isla had to get rid of them and she saved everyone. The witch disappeared eventually.

Alicia Popps (9)
Luddendenfoot Academy, Luddendenfoot

THE BOY IN THE SCHOOL

Emily looked at the old, creepy school. She wondered what it looked like in 1973 in the back of her mind. Emily was silent before she screamed at the top of her voice at the sight of a boy covered in blood, coming from the school.
When she stopped screaming, the boy looked at her creepily. She just stood there for a minute, then she ran for dear life. As she was running, the boy teleported in front of her, so she ran back to the school to stay safe. She was safe for now, she just stood there...

Maisie Hayes (9)
Luddendenfoot Academy, Luddendenfoot

HEADLESS HORSEMAN

One day, Henry went horse riding in the dark and hit his head on a branch. His head flew off and fire came out of his neck. Now, if you go there, people say he will kill you. He likes to haunt the field at night. The field is full of green, sticky grass that grabs your legs when you walk through it and you can hear his old victims screaming in the wind. All you will see as he comes to kill you is hot, burning fire and a terrifying, red-eyed, giant horse. Be very, very careful outside...

Lucas Stringer (10)
Luddendenfoot Academy, Luddendenfoot

THE GIRL IN THE DRESS

I was sat in my bedroom, watching TV, and all of a sudden there was a knock at the window. I went up to the window, but there was nothing there, so I sat back down on my bed. I had a feeling someone was watching me.
The next day, the same thing happened to me again, but I knew there was someone there, definitely. After a few hours, there was a face at the window. It was a girl with a long fringe. I went to help her and fell through her! I lay there, my spine had broken!

Lucy Smith (10)
Luddendenfoot Academy, Luddendenfoot

THE SPOOKY SLAPPY BOY

One stormy night, I was watching TV when my friend came in saying that something was chasing her. The thing that was chasing her was a ghost boy! He slapped me on the cheek and again and again. I threw him out of the window, then we ran for it. I found a tree house in the deep, dark woods. We hid for a bit. Inside, it was very smelly and old. The ghost passed us and we ran home. We watched an old horror movie.

Ella Brooks (9)
Luddendenfoot Academy, Luddendenfoot

THE ROOM

When I woke up, I was in a different place, a very different place. "Where am I?"
After thirty seconds, I heard an unfamiliar voice. Before my operation, the only thing I remembered was the whispering voice of my mother giving me good luck. But, that wasn't my mother. "Welcome to the room," groaned a voice.
The room? I thought. Petrified, sweating, I tried to run anywhere I could, but I'd had an operation on my legs so I couldn't move. As the voice got louder, I realised the person speaking was in my mind. Everything was my imagination...

Jessica Schofield (10)
Manston Primary School, Crossgates

THE DARK FIGURE

All of a sudden, Lily yelled because something had pulled on her hair. She realised that she was all by herself in the mansion... "Mum!" she screamed.
No answer. She ran as fast as she could, straight to her bedroom and hid under her bed.
"I will find you!" shouted a dark figure lurking outside Lily's bedroom.
Lily started to cry out, "Who are you?"
"Hannah," the figure said. "I'm dead. Do you remember me from reception?"
"No," Lily said, not realising that would be her last word...

Lily Swordy (10)
Manston Primary School, Crossgates

LOCK YOUR DOORS

One night, on Knightsway, Charlie, Mum and Dad were building a den. Last year, they'd gotten a message from an unknown person saying, 'I know where you live. Just remember: lock your doors'. Now, the family kept the doors locked at all times and they slept together just to be safe. "Knock, knock!" shouted a voice.
It came from the closet. Charlie went to inspect it, but a voice came from behind him. "Would you like to sleep?" the voice whispered.
And, just like that, little Charlie and his family were no longer screaming...

Harley James Dews (10)
Manston Primary School, Crossgates

THE STRANGER

One day, I was hanging out with my friend. I saw a white van. I said, "Did you see that?" She just laughed and said, "See what?"

I thought that it was weird, but then I started to walk home. I saw the white van behind me. I thought, *who could this be following me? Who could this be?* I began to run home. I looked behind me, nobody was there. I thought to myself, *better run home quickly.*

My mum and dad weren't at home. I tried to unlock the door, it wouldn't work. I saw the white van...

Leah Badcock (11)
Manston Primary School, Crossgates

THE BANG

Running upstairs to her room was Gracie. After a long day at the doctors about her broken arm, she was exhausted. That night, she had been left home alone while her mum went to the shop to get some tea. Once she got to her room, she started to paint her nails.
Quickly running downstairs to lock the door, she heard a bang that came from her mum's bedroom. She ran back to her bedroom, trying to look around the corner at her mum's room. She heard a deep voice say, "Finally, you've locked the door. We are alone now."

Lilly Holliday (11)
Manston Primary School, Crossgates

THE WINTER NIGHT

It was a cold winter's night; I was walking my dog. My phone began to ring, but it was a tune I had never heard before. When I grabbed it out of my pocket, it was a random number. I answered. They said, "I will get you."
I hung up. When I got home, I shouted to Mum to tell her, but she wasn't there so I shouted for Dad. He didn't answer so I searched for them. Where had they gone? Minutes later, the door opened. *Creak!* It was Mum and Dad! They were home! *Phew!* They were safe!

Gracie Leigh Partner (11)
Manston Primary School, Crossgates

FIGURE IN THE WOODS

Walking back from a huge party, Noah was very tired as it was just about midnight. He was fifteen at the time and was very happy because he'd finally had the nerve to ask out Nancy. She had said yes.
Noah was tired, he took a shortcut through the woods. All of a sudden, Noah saw a slim, dark figure. Fear struck his heart as it followed him. His home was nearby. The thing came closer and closer, Noah noticed it was his friend. He'd come to tell him that Nancy was thinking about going to Nando's tomorrow!

Oliver Moran (11)
Manston Primary School, Crossgates

THE SHADOW

Mike had just come back from work and his only intention was to go to bed. He trudged up the stairs, trying his best not to fall or drop his briefcase. Mike dropped the files and paperwork spread across the passage floor; a sharp knock echoed through the halls. He dashed down the stairs and peered through the eyehole. He saw nothing. He opened the door, then closed it again. Something felt different, the lights were on and he hadn't tinkered with anything when he came home. The light went off, he wasn't alone...

Kasseykylie Kucherera (11)
Manston Primary School, Crossgates

ALWAYS ALONE

I was alone and cold; my parents had gone out to London. I was terrified. I didn't know what to do. Suddenly, I heard a loud noise. *Bang!* I hid under the blanket. My mum and dad had told me not to be afraid of anything. Bravely, I crept up the creaking stairs. I peeked around the bathroom door. "Hello," a creepy voice whispered.
"Hello?" I muttered.
The door slammed behind me. *Bang!* "No one is going to save you; your parents aren't alive!"

Mia Wood (11)
Manston Primary School, Crossgates

THE STALKER IN THE WOODS

Two boys were in the woods and they didn't know what time it was, so they went further. They saw a body. They turned around to go home but a little voice said, "Want to play hide-and-seek?"

Out of the bushes came a figure with a kitchen knife. Their mum went to the woods where they usually played and, when she went further into the woods, she saw them lying dead on the floor. She called the ambulance and, while she called them, she realised that she wasn't alone...

Tyler Emmett (10)
Manston Primary School, Crossgates

...ME MAN

I woke up and heard a car engine. At first, I thought it was my dad, but no, it was a man, a suspicious-looking man in a suspicious-looking vehicle. Then, I looked away to ask my mum if she knew him. She said no.
Suddenly, we heard a bang downstairs, like breaking glass. I'd seen his face somewhere before, but I couldn't remember it. All of a sudden, I remembered something on the news about a robber. Then, I realised that he was robbing us. I hid under my bed with my mum...

Thomas Kilcoyne (10)
Manston Primary School, Crossgates

THE TERRIBLE VIRUS

It spread like gossip. The terrible virus picked off everyone one by one. Jack, who was a young boy, ran swiftly through the dark and sinister forest, trying to keep away from the evil, malicious zombies. The virus was an experiment that went terribly wrong and spread around the world. Jack was one of the only people who hadn't been infected.
The zombies were coming from everywhere. It was terrible. Athletic Jack sprinted for his life and didn't intend on stopping. The horrible creatures circled around him and sprang upon him. The world was doomed: everyone was infected...

Sameer Ayub (10)
Parkinson Lane Community Primary School, Halifax

. DOLL

ɔpened the broken doorknob with my shaking ıand. Tears cascaded down my red cheeks, I walked across the creaky floorboards, leading to the haunting stairs. I hesitated to go up them. I was shackled by fear, but I put it to a side and bravely went up the stairs.
There was a room which I went into. Unusually, it opened by itself. Scary voodoo dolls were drawn on the wrinkled wallpaper. I looked ahead of me. A girl with black eyes stared into my soul, holding a doll, head at a 90° angle. *Goodbye my friends,* I thought.

Maleeha Naz (10)
Parkinson Lane Community Primary School, Halifax

WATCH OUT!

Silence filled the room as the darkness took one step forward every minute. Questions rummaged around my head like, 'where am I?' and 'how did I get here?' My voice turned down as an unknown figure crept secretly behind me. I reluctantly turned around as black spiders wiggled their legs around the attic. A shovel was revealed in the light.
Closer and closer it crept. My heart was pumping fast, I was so scared. I saw a face. It was Dad! "There you are, I thought you were lost!"
"Were you hiding, Dad?"

Haniya Dawood (8)
Parkinson Lane Community Primary School, Halifax

'OOKY MURDER!

There I lay in curiosity, but in fear at the .e time. I didn't know where I was or what do because, at that moment, I had just eard a creepy, whispering voice: "I'm coming to get you!"
These few words chilled me to the very bone. Trembling shakily, I slowly walked towards the cupboard where the noise was coming from. There I gazed suspiciously until I saw a huge eyeball popping out of a jar! Quaking in fear, I tried to hide, but it was too late. The cold, powerful wind grabbed me by the neck...

Bisma Moghul (11)
Parkinson Lane Community Primary School, Halifax

THE SPOOKY HALLOWEEN

I lie in my cosy bedroom, reading a spooky Halloween magazine when a terrifying flash of lightning hits my eyes and everything dims. I creep under my blanket and, to my surprise, I hear an eerie crackle coming from the window.
I lie still. "Who's there?"
I turn slowly to see a dark shadow lurking over me. I try to scream, but with no sound. I'm petrified and my heart is beating louder. I notice a hand coming closer. I try to run, but it's too late...
I take a closer look and it's my naughty brother.

Falak Arshid (8)
Parkinson Lane Community Primary School, Halifax

...D THE WHISPERING MONSTERS

... came around. Night had come since I'd ... Where was I? Where could I go? I was in ...unted house, the dull wallpaper peeling off ... top of me. Suddenly, there were whispering ...oices. I ran. I didn't look back at all.
...hen, I turned around and took a deep breath.
I said, "Hello? Anybody there?"
But, all of a sudden, I saw somebody lingering over me. I tried to scream, but I couldn't. I was terrified, full of fear. I took a moment to catch my breath, but then it was only my dad!

Maryam Bibi (8)
Parkinson Lane Community Primary School, Halifax

WHO IS THIS MAN?

We recently moved into a new creepy-looking house. When we pulled up in our driveway, I saw a mysterious figure standing in the attic window. I hoped that wasn't my bedroom. I walked into the new house and started to explore. I couldn't find anything until I came across a beaten-down, old door. I was guessing that was the attic. My parents told me that was my new room.

As I was getting ready for bed, I heard a noise coming from under my bed. Then I saw the mysterious figure standing there... Who was he?

Ibrahim Rasul (8)

Parkinson Lane Community Primary School, Halifax

...ND THE HAUNTED HOUSE

...iere was a boy called Ralph. He lived by ...f, alone at home. Ralph saw a haunted ...e. He wondered what was in there. ... day, Ralph saw an ancient man go inside. ...lph went inside the haunted house too. ...Vhen Ralph walked inside, he saw the ancient man. Ralph went into a room in the haunted house and saw a picture of a ghost! The windows shut, the door shut. The ghost was red and pushed Ralph onto the floor. Ralph rushed home and stayed there. The ghost was waiting for Ralph to come back again...

Hudaifa Ali (9)
Parkinson Lane Community Primary School, Halifax

THE SOUNDS OF THE SPOOKY HOUSE

I was in an ancient, abandoned house. Everything was silent until I heard whispers lurking about. I gulped in fear and a shiver ran down my spine. The darkness innundated me, I could hear the haunting whispers coming from the mouth of the house. It got to the point where the silent whispers deafened me. The high-pitched shriek was unbearable. I covered my ears, yet nothing stopped it from coming. Suddenly, I woke up, feeling startled, with sweat upon my brow. I checked my alarm clock which read 4.03am...

Fizah Junaid (10)
Parkinson Lane Community Primary School, Halifax

THE SINISTER SLEEPOVER

Finally, the day has come! Only two hours until Mum drops me off at Kendall's house for her birthday sleepover everyone's been waiting for! We're all extremely excited, only ten minutes now!
After a twenty-five minute drive, we're here!
Three hours later, everyone's asleep. It seems kind of creepy and frightening alone. Suddenly, the doors start creaking. Kendall's mansion is definitely haunted.
A few minutes later, the lights start flickering and then, outside, Kendall's mum's car alarm starts roaring! I can't handle this anymore, so I open my mouth wide to scream, "Argh! Help!"

Lucy Harper (10)
Primrose Lane Primary School, Boston Spa

LOCKED IN

Where was I? How did I get here? I didn't know how, but here I was, locked in the dark, creepy house. I could hear his footsteps approaching. I looked up and saw his evil eyes.
I ran up the stairs, but there was no escape. I could feel him getting closer, so I ran faster, but I fell. I felt a hand on my shoulder. "Get up!" he shouted, but I squeezed my eyes shut, tighter.
"Get up." His voice softened, so I slowly opened my eyes.
"You've been dreaming for ages," said my mum.

Maryam Yasin (7)
Pudsey Bolton Royd Primary School, Pudsey

HALLOWEEN SPOOKY NIGHTMARE TRICK

It was Halloween night, the clock struck nine o'clock and a family were out trick or treating. Suddenly, *bang!* There was a witch outside a house. "Who goes there?"
They left. The next thing they knew, the two children were found dead. "Oh no!" the parents cried. "Help!"
Luckily, the witch gave them a potion. Little did people know that the witch wasn't a witch, she was dressed up! The family found out and they gave the children the potion. The children woke up and the family bought a new house away from there.

Laibah-Amina Hussain (9)
Ravensthorpe CE (VC) Junior School, Ravensthorpe

THE SURGEON

I daringly ran to the biggest house on my street: the surgeon's. I took a deep breath and knocked. The door swung open. I stepped in. It was like I was in a trance. I was walking step by step, my legs trembling, my heart pounding. Then, my whole body froze. A tall silhouette edged towards me. The surgeon was here. I felt like I was paralysed, I couldn't move. The surgeon muttered four words, "I'm gonna dissect you!"
She grasped her scalpel. I screamed and ran to the door and, as soon as I was free, the house disappeared...

Simran Shakoor (10)
Ravensthorpe CE (VC) Junior School, Ravensthorpe

BLACK DEATH

Night had fallen, it was pitch-black outside, but the moon still shone brightly. The clock struck nine o'clock so I ran upstairs into my bedroom. Everything went black.
I woke up and happened to be in an old haunted house. Suddenly, a witch caught my eye. She was holding a black apple. I wanted to hide but, when I did, she grabbed me as quickly as she could. Shivers shot up my spine and I felt paralysed. Immediately, I decided to face my fears and kicked the witch.
Finally, I shoved the apple into her mouth. She then fell...

Rida Rehman (9)
Ravensthorpe CE (VC) Junior School, Ravensthorpe

The Out-Of-This-World Circus Tickets!

"Don't buy the tickets!" bellowed the tramp. Following a day searching for the circus that didn't exist, we felt like foolish clowns. From my window, I admired the Statue of Liberty through the smog. Suddenly, the statue grew red hair and red boots! "Look!" I yelled to my friends.

They saw nothing. The television crime report switched to juggling balls raining onto criminals, car chases by police riding circus bikes and blowing party whistles! Roads transformed into undrivable tightropes. The sky became one gloomy big top. The out-of-this-world circus was here. "Ready or not, here I come..."

Tiffany Robson (10)
Saltersgate Junior School, Scawsby

I SEE YOU!

It was foggy all around, I could barely see anything. Suddenly, thunder and lightning appeared, then rain started to slowly pour down on my sweaty face. In the long distance, I heard a deafening noise that sounded like a signal, but I wasn't too sure.

As I lingered in the bush, I tried to pull myself together and see where I was. *What?* There was that abnormal sound again... Wait... "I see you."

Who? Who can see me? By this point, I was holding back my tears. Just as I turned around... "Argh! Who are you?"

Olivia Hardy (11)

Saltersgate Junior School, Scawsby

A DREARY NIGHT

Darkness falls; all the lights have blown, the only light is from the moon and stars and even that isn't bright enough as the mist blocks most of it. I walk into the kitchen - plates, glasses, bowls and mugs smashed on the floor which is, for some reason, dusty, as well as scattered cutlery everywhere. I'd locked the door before I'd left, how could anyone get in? Calming myself, I go upstairs to rest. Lights flash eerily. I see a greying figure, she seems dead. This must be the culprit.
I awaken, it was a dream. Or was it?

Phoebe Cooper (11)
Saltersgate Junior School, Scawsby

HORROR HOUSE

One Halloween, me and Sam saw a strange, abandoned house. We decided to look inside, so we opened the old, wooden door.
Terrifyingly, I saw groaning, creepy zombies. They shuffled closer until we were stuck in front of the peeling wall.
We quickly ran right into something freezing cold! We looked up and realised it was a vampire! I grabbed Sam and ran as fast as we could until we were on the street. Sam was pale, dripping with sweat and exclaimed, "That's the last time I follow you anywhere!"
Soon, the sunrise came and the vampires and zombies disappeared...

Scarlett Anne Pattinson (8)
Southroyd Primary School, Pudsey

THE FIGURE

Me and my dad moved into a new house. I went exploring. I came across a big wardrobe with a mirror on the door. Amazingly, I had no reflection! I put my hand on the mirror to find my hand went straight through it. I went through the mirror and saw a dark, sinister forest.

A shadow was in the distance. I walked further into the forest to hide, but the shadow followed me. I looked everywhere for the wardrobe, but it wasn't there. The shadow was coming closer. I didn't know what to do. Closer... Quicker... It was here!

Connor Reece Kisby (9)
Southroyd Primary School, Pudsey

THERE'S A GOBLIN IN MY HOUSE

Hi, my name's Maurice and there are goblins in my house. I don't know why.
I haven't called the police either. They probably won't believe me, so I close the door and I can hear them jumping up and down on the floor.
This is probably against the law.
My cat won't even go near the door and my roommate screams loudly when he sees them.
We go downstairs and see that, unfortunately, in the bathroom, there's another goblin. I say,
"Don't you dare!"
They all run out the door!

Jamie Lucas O'Brien (8)
Southroyd Primary School, Pudsey

FRANKENSTEIN'S HOUSE

As blood dripped down the wall, a ghost hovered above me. I turned around to get closer to the kitchen, so I could escape through the back door. Then, a zombie stopped me in my tracks and ran towards me viciously. Soon, I ran to the front door, but Frankenstein was there. I figured out that it must be Frankenstein's house, all the clues added up: a zombie, a ghost and a really tall house.
As I made my way to the second floor, a vampire led me to a vicious trap. I knew it was Frankenstein's house!

Jayden Barraclough (8)
Southroyd Primary School, Pudsey

A FRIGHTENING NIGHT

I looked up at the black sky. I hadn't intended to be out this late. The sun had set and the empty road ahead had no streetlights. I knew I was in for a dark journey home. I had decided that travelling through the forest would be the quickest way home.
Minutes passed, yet it seemed like hours and days. The further I travelled into the forest, the darker it seemed to get. I began to whistle to take my mind off the eerie noises I was hearing. I took a glance around to see little eyes looking at me...

Evie Mason (9)
Southroyd Primary School, Pudsey

WEIRD TRICK-OR-TREATERS

Once upon a time, a trick-or-treater was going to a creepy house and she had facepaint all over her eyes. She was creepy and mean. She got to the door.

When she opened the door, there was a dark figure behind her. She dropped all of her sweets, they went all over the floor. The dark figure jumped out of the shadows. It was just her dad!

She and her dad had dinner, but she was scared of monsters in her room, so she went to bed with her dad. She then went to sleep...

Rose Janani (8)
Southroyd Primary School, Pudsey

THE UNKNOWN

It was a cold, dark night and Joe was running wildly. Heart pounding, he stumbled through the eerie graveyard, wishing this nightmare would end. *Wait... What was that?*
Joe's strides became bigger as he could make out a small, black figure looming towards him. Suddenly, all went silent. Joe felt like the world had stopped, except for him and this strange figure. Lots of unanswered thoughts raced through his mind. *Why am I here? Why on Halloween?*
Finally, everything zoned back into motion. By this time, the mysterious shape was right next to him. There was a shrill scream...

Ebony Dickinson (10)
St Michael's CE Primary School, Dalston

THE GHOST

Dad was driving me home one night and we picked up a pale lady wearing all white, she was hitchhiking. She didn't speak the whole time, she just stared out of the frosty window; we didn't know where she was going. Something felt odd.

As we passed the abandoned graveyard, she disappeared into thin air. *Was it a ghost?* I suddenly thought. We arrived home at midnight; I went straight to bed. Whilst closing my flimsy curtains, I saw a figure floating outside. It was the ghost we'd seen earlier! Frozen with fear, I slowly walked to my comforting bed...

Lucy Olivia Bowie (10)
St Michael's CE Primary School, Dalston

THE NIGHT BEFORE HALLOWEEN

James' heart pounded like a drum. He felt as if it might burst out of his chest. A strange tapping noise was coming from the window. He then heard whispering. His candle flickered and went out as if someone had blown on it. Footsteps edged towards him as he lit his candle once more.

A dark figure loomed over him. He then screamed a shrill scream, dropped his candle and woke up in a cold sweat to find his candle unlit in his gloomy, moonlit bedroom. It was Halloween. James pinched himself in case he was still in the nightmare...

Megan Smith (11)
St Michael's CE Primary School, Dalston

JASMINE THE TEENAGE WITCH

Inspired by 'Chilling Adventures of Sabrina'

It was the day before Halloween. Jasmine still hadn't made a decision on whether to stay mortal or be a proper witch. Jasmine went to the candy store to get some candy for her Halloween party. She handed the money over, skipping to her Halloween party.

It was Halloween. Her aunty Sandra said, "Get this dress on!"

She refused and wore her mother's wedding dress. It was twelve at night. She walked through the forest and killed a priest. She decided to stay mortal. That night, she was haunted by Mr Unknown, a black abyss. Anything could happen next...

Ellie Baimbridge (10)

St Patrick's Catholic Primary School, Elland

A SPOOKY HALLOWEEN

There were three trick-or-treaters and they knocked on one house. Someone whispered, "Come in."
They walked in and, *bang!* The door shut behind them. There was a faint scream, "Argh!" Someone said, "Hello?"
One of the trick-or-treaters started crying. The doors started opening and closing. *Bang! Bang! Bang!* They all started crying! "Waa!"
"Ssh!" one of them whispered.
"I can hear you!" a nun said.
"Run!"
The nun started chasing them. One got eaten alive and the other people were never seen again. They didn't end up getting any sweets...

Alfie Hunter (10)
St Patrick's CE Primary School, Endmoor

THE GLOOMY GRAVEYARD

"What on..." Evelyn jolted awake. She looked out of the grimy, cracked window. It turned out that she was in a deserted graveyard; all the graves were covered in moss. She was sure she'd fallen asleep in her own bed.
Suddenly, one grave started glowing and a sinister figure rose out of the gloom. Slowly, he approached Evelyn and circled her, his face showing an angry expression. "Why are you here?" Evelyn demanded.
He answered in an audible growl. She thought he was half-man, half-bear. He came closer and knocked Evelyn unconscious. He stood there, drooling over her...

Erin Munford (9)
St Patrick's CE Primary School, Endmoor

MUSEUM MAYHEM

Bertie and Wendy Hallows entered the mythical museum. It was the dead of night as they crept into another section, but were horrified that they had entered the haunted house. Before they could do anything, they were swept up in a black whirlwind...
Landing with a bump, they blinked to find themselves in a wooden house. Spying a zombie, they ran off to escape. Panting, Wendy pressed herself against a spiky wall that sent exaggerated shivers up her spine. *Slam!* The door shut. She raced to catch her breath as she saw a zombie with a threatening knife. "No! Argh!"

Bethany Taylor (11)
St Patrick's CE Primary School, Endmoor

THE HAUNTED CHEERIOS

I walked down the stairs for breakfast. As I brought the Cheerios down from the shelf, I fell off the stool.
When I woke, everything was the same apart from all the food had been replaced with strangely coloured, bubbling liquids in jars. Wondering what was in the jars, I noticed some had beige labels, saying things like 'fried toenails' next to 'rat livers' and 'boiled throats'. As I walked, a mysterious figure loomed over me. Everything went black. White writing appeared, reading 'to be continued'. *Phew!* It was just the TV...

Oliver Sanday (10)
St Patrick's CE Primary School, Endmoor

THE NIGHT-TIME TERROR

Finally, a new day in a new town. It was a dull town, but strange. In my room, it was about 9pm, almost bedtime. "Ethan," someone whispered in a faint, croaky voice.
"Hello? Mum? Dad? Who's there?"
My closet door opened. A girl was standing there with a bruise on her neck and blood dripping from her mouth. I was frozen in fear. I was paralysed. It felt like the ghost wanted me to join her. It said, "Ethan, I want my heart back. I am under your bed..."
She disappeared... The next minute, I heard a bang!

Ethan Kearsley (10)
St Patrick's CE Primary School, Endmoor

TRICK OR TREAT HORROR

Alice and Fred were trick or treating. When they got to one house, the door slowly creaked open. They could hear voices of past residents of the house. They entered a room that looked like an attic. The next thing they knew, there was a hand pushing them into a cupboard. It was pitch-black. There was a figure moving towards them. There was a feeling that these were their last moments that they would see. But, it wasn't. The homeowners found them lying there. They called the police, who took them to the hospital where their parents were waiting...

Rhys Newby-Bush (10)
St Patrick's CE Primary School, Endmoor

THE GIANT GRAVESTONE

There I was, trembling with fear, holding a rotten, golden doorhandle, standing in an abandoned graveyard. I'd had enough. The door creaked open. I stood, staring at another door, but this one was covered with sticky goo. Suddenly, the door slammed shut. Only then did I notice spiders on the floor. I rushed to the next room. Slime trickled down my fingertips. Another door, this one was covered in blood and cobwebs. Out of nowhere, a vent opened and out came two ghosts. *Quick! Next door!* The blood touched me. I saw a gravestone...

Daniel Horrigan (10)
St Patrick's CE Primary School, Endmoor

KNOCK, KNOCK!

I woke up. It was 11.59pm. Silence ran through the house. There was just enough light for me to see the room. Suddenly, there was a knock, it came from the cupboard. I lay there, still, not moving a muscle. *Knock! Knock!*
I heard footsteps coming upstairs. *Knock!* The stairs started creaking, the footsteps got louder and louder. I heard a grunt. Whoever it was was outside my door. Then, slowly, the door creaked open. I shut my eyes a little, but I could still see. His heavy boots banged against the floor... It was Santa!

Jess Wilson (11)
St Patrick's CE Primary School, Endmoor

THE GHOST

In a haunted house lived Ben and Benji with zombies! A horrible monster lurked in the darkness, ready to pounce and drag mortals into an abyss of death, stealing your life and destroying you completely. It lived in their house, but it never came out.
But one night, it crawled out of its home, the attic. The sound was horrifying and creepy, but it ran away, back to its hiding place, because it was morning. It was light, which was its weakness. Finally, Ben and Benji knew its weakness, that meant they could use it to defeat it.

Ben Morris (9)
St Patrick's CE Primary School, Endmoor

THE CUPBOARD OF WHISPERS

I walked into the house that looked like mine. Then, a doll sitting on a windowsill woke up and ran at me and whispered, "Come with me," under her breath.
I followed, feeling petrified. I stepped into a room, my heart pounding. She sat me in a seat and went away. I sat there silently, staring at the floor. She came back and turned on the light, it started to flicker. When the light was on, she was there; the light went off and back on. She was gone. I ran into a cupboard, startled. I could hear her whispering...

Ella Allan (10)
St Patrick's CE Primary School, Endmoor

THE DEADLY GHOST

The day was finally here. I got to go to a mansion. "Let's go!"
I eventually got there. I was so excited. Then, when I got in my room, I put the light on and it turned off, then on, then stopped! I was spooked out! Later on, I went to make myself a sandwich. When I got everything out, it all moved to the top of the cupboard! I was so scared! Then, spiders and blood dripped all over me. I started to scream.
After that, I went into the bathroom and saw a ghost! I screamed and fainted...

Abby Mason (10)
St Patrick's CE Primary School, Endmoor

THE COAL HOUSE PHANTOM...

Once, my grandad caught a prisoner trying to escape, so he locked her in the coal house. She cast a phantom on him. Later, he was found dead in the coal house...
It was back! It was only me, abandoned in the house, when all of a sudden it sounded like a ball and chain was in the wall. I stumbled to the coal house where the walls were accessible. White ectoplasm covered the walls, chains rattled all around me, then I saw a dark figure in front of me. I was chained to the wall, slowly drowning in coal...

Nathan Barnabas Galbraith (10)
St Patrick's CE Primary School, Endmoor

THE VICTORIAN GHOST

There was once a house that nobody lived in. The reason nobody lived in it was because it was full of Victorian ghosts. You could always hear them surrounding you. Sometimes you could see the faint air of them moving. They were the worst of all the horrible, scary monsters.

One day, a little girl saw one of the ghosts. She quickly ran inside as fast as a cheetah and told her parents, but unfortunately, they didn't believe her. The next day, she went to the house and never returned...

Sophie Tubbs (9)

St Patrick's CE Primary School, Endmoor

THE WALK THAT WENT WRONG

One night, I went out for a walk with my dog, Benji, when we bumped into a volcano. So, we went to find the door and, when we went in, I saw a dead body. Benji the dog licked the blood off the body. The door creaked closed and, when I turned around, there were dark figures looking at me. There was a vampire and a zombie.
They chased me, so I got into a cupboard. There were nine coming towards us. The last thing we saw was a zombie. We were killed!

William Taylor (9)
St Patrick's CE Primary School, Endmoor

IT

Midnight, I'm awake, I'm scared. I don't think they heard the creaking sound downstairs. Have you heard it? There it is again... *Creak!* What should I do? Go back to sleep? Have a look? *Creak!* It's coming closer, whatever IT is. Fear is pumping through my body. My hairs stand on edge. There it is again... *Creak!* Right outside my room. I shudder, I quiver and bury myself under the duvet. I inhale deeply. "It's nothing," I tell myself, but there it is again. *Creak!* The door opens. There IT is. I force my eyes open. IT has found me...

Charlotte Olivia Hawkin (11)
Three Lane Ends Academy, Castleford

THE TRANQUILISER AND A HAUNTED HOUSE

On Halloween night, there was a five-year-old girl going trick or treating. Her name was Zoey. She knocked on one door that was really suspicious. When she knocked on it and a portal appeared, it sucked her all the way to a haunted house!

Zoey knocked on the door and it creaked open. No one was there. She went inside. She looked around and no one was there. All of a sudden, Zoey turned around and there she saw Caspar the evil ghost. The evil ghost, Casper, went up to Zoey and tried to tranquilise her!

Loretta Knott (9)
West Road Primary School, Moorends

THE ALIVE SPOOKY CASTLE

Once upon a time, there was a witch who lived in a spooky castle and she was called Saga. One day, she felt lonely, so she tried to make a poison to make another person. Suddenly, a bottle broke. Saga realised it was a potion to make things come alive!
All of a sudden, the castle started moving to a different place! All was quiet. Out of nowhere, there was a big bang on the door. Who could it be? Then, after that, the castle stopped moving and there was a dark shadow behind her. Oh no...

Milena Bury (9)
West Road Primary School, Moorends

YOUNG WRITERS INFORMATION

We hope you have enjoyed reading this book – and that you will continue to in the coming years.

If you're a young writer who enjoys reading and creative writing, or the parent of an enthusiastic poet or story writer, do visit our website **www.youngwriters.co.uk**. Here you will find free competitions, workshops and games, as well as recommended reads, a poetry glossary and our blog. There's lots to keep budding writers motivated to write!

If you would like to order further copies of this book, or any of our other titles, then please give us a call or order via your online account.

Young Writers
Remus House
Coltsfoot Drive
Peterborough
PE2 9BF
(01733) 890066
info@youngwriters.co.uk

Join in the conversation!
Tips, news, giveaways and much more!

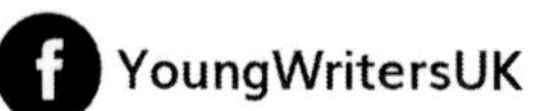